Hidden

Amelia J Hunter

Leigh
Thank you for
all your hard work
making my book
pretty.
amelia

Dedication

To the country that adopted me, the man who married me, and the Irish mother who raised me.

The Start of the End

Samuel froze. The three-wheeled car he had stopped rolling up the back of the couch shook in his small, dirty hand, his heartbeat pumping through his chest. Whoever was hammering on the front door seemed desperate to enter, but this wasn't the time for visitors. The sun was still trying to creep in through the tattered curtains and his tummy hadn't growled yet.

With not much furniture in the room, the only place he could hide was on the other side of the couch, under the coffee table whose missing glass had been replaced with a sheet of board. This wasn't the first time he'd needed to take cover and he knew he could make the jump before all hell broke loose. His thin frame made him a fast mover when he had to be, but the banging on the door had increased to a relentless hammering and it had frozen him.

A trickle of pee started to slide down the inside of his leg, and instinctively, he held onto himself to stop any more from escaping, using a few words that were wrong for his age of seven years. Now was not a good time for him to be weak, so he fought back the tears that were trying to break free. Closing his eyes tightly, he wished and hoped that whoever was on the other side of the front door wouldn't wake the woman upstairs.

His young brain told him he had no choice but to hide. He had to move and now. When he released his hold, the flow had been stemmed long enough to jump over the back of the seat and swiftly dive under the table, dropping his favourite car on the way in his hurry. Lying with his cheek on the floor, watching the gap where the sitting room door used to open into the hall, he tucked his gangling legs into his chest, staying as still as his trembling body would allow.

The stench of filth filled his nostrils; he hated this patterned carpet, never managing to avoid the dark patches that increased every few days. He struggled to hold his breath for as long as he could, and his stomach turned the moment he had no choice but to pull in a reluctant gasp. He spat the bile from his mouth into a burnt hole in the carpet near a rusty brown diamond shape before holding his breath again and waiting.

The ruckus from the front door suddenly quieted, allowing a deafening silence to hang in the air. His heart fought hard to stay in his chest.

Carefully, he poked his head out from his hiding place, keeping his eyes locked on where the door should have been. From the position he was in, he wouldn't be able to see who wanted to come into the house – he would have to look through the window for that – but the last two stairs were visible.

Taking in a large gulp of musty air, his skinny chest heaved in and out, showing his rips like a rack on a plate. His heart heaved and he panted heavily, making him thirsty and leaving a dead taste in his mouth.

Sometimes he liked the silence. To him, the silence meant he would be left alone to play with the small metal cars that some of the guests gave him. The ones who patted his head on the way upstairs were the kindest, even if their faces didn't show it. He thought of the one in particular who gave him a fistful of jelly sweets as *the woman* waited at the top of the stairs. It was their secret and he'd held on tight to his gift so *she* wouldn't see as the man passed him. That man was the kindest, and right then, he would have loved to have those jellies in his hand.

Today, though, the silence was different.

A gentle knock on the glass window startled him and he banged his back off the wood overlapping the table frame in fright. Biting his lip so as not to vocalise the throbbing pain, he cranked his head towards the curtain. In their sorrowful state, they swayed slightly from the breeze coming in through the crack in the top corner that had widened recently, and slowly, he lowered himself back to his haven in a ball.

A bellowing female voice shouted through the

7

letterbox. The urgency in the woman's words indicated that he couldn't have been seen, but what control he had over his bladder disappeared. This was not going to be a good day for him when his mother found out.

From the floor above him, a door banged loudly with enough force to dislodge more of the loose plaster off the hallway wall, making the hole even bigger. Slow feet dragged along the lino floor, indicating that she was wearing the grey slippers with no backs on, the ones she pushed her oversized feet into. Whoever woke *her* up will get a telling off. He smiled at the thought, knowing, this time, it wasn't him. As he waited under the coffee table to see the tips of the slippers at the bottom of the stairs, he calculated how fast he would need to be to skim past her and up the stairs so he could strip off his wet pyjamas before she smelled the pee. Her reflexes were better than those of any rugby player he had seen on the telly catching a ball from the air, and he dreaded her catching him. Considering her rounded size, he was surprised she managed to move at all, but she could when she needed to.

He thought about blaming the dog he used to own for the stain on the floor. His little companion's ears would point upwards when *she* woke. His tail would dip between his back legs, and no matter what game they were playing at the time, Bud would dive under the coffee table, the same way Samuel had just done. It was during one of those times that the table had been broken, but he didn't want to think of that now. He needed to keep his focus on those steps.

It always amazed him that *she* could somehow pinpoint his wrongdoing while the rest of the place was in such a mess. *She* never blamed the smell on the food that was stuck on the plates in the sink for days, or the toilet that was always blocked after a busy night. No, everything that needed blame had his name all over it.

But this time, it wasn't him that had woken her.

He stretched his arm out for his favourite red car. The paint had worn off a long time ago, but in Samuel's mind, the car must have been red. He grasped it in his unwashed hand and tucked it into his damp pyjama pants. His eyes darted from his hiding place around the room, thinking what else he needed to keep safe before the rampage began and he had to make a run for it. Nothing but a piece of string caught his eye. The thread hanging from the tattered brown couch was one of his favourites. Many days and evenings he would sit on the cushion, his legs reaching the floor due to the lack of springs in the couch, threading the dusky grey thread through his fingers. The string gave him comfort, blanking everything else happening in the house from his thoughts. He hid it under the loose cushion when he didn't need it, but it must have got free when he jumped over the chair. The last time *she* was in a foul mood, the house had been tipped upside down and he'd lost a piece of cord he loved so much, it took days afterwards to find a replacement.

With the shouting continuing through the letterbox in the hallway and the sound of the toilet flushing above him, he quickly left his safe place. His heart pounded so fast he hoped it would stay in his chest. Running over to the chair, he pulled the thread with all his might but even though the fabric was worn, it wouldn't break free. Wetting his lips, he leaned closer and with his small teeth, he tugged tight until it snapped, making him stumble a little. Quickly, on his hands and knees, he crawled back to his haven as he heard the first of her steps on the creaky stairs.

Slowly he twisted the thread around the top of his index finger, tightening it with each twirl. He blanked out the shouting match as his mother's footsteps reached the last few steps. Instead, he watched as the tip of his finger began to swell and glow red. His empty stomach called out for the food he had missed, yet again, but even that didn't deter him from the intensity he felt from his own doing.

He smiled and waited.

Soon, he would feel the rush of blood when he let the tension go.

Soon, the small bit of control he had over his life would flow through him.

Soon, he would miss his chance to run behind her to change his clothes.

Soon, things would change.

Soon.

One

Dark hair, curled from sweat, stuck to the forehead of the restless man. Side to side, his head tossed in quick succession, eyes tightly closed. His broad chest caved deeper, exhaling a groan from deep within his throat, his breathing laboured. Beneath him, the sheet was damp from the tremors trapped and left implanted on the grey cotton.

This wasn't the first time his body had given way to his early morning fears, but it was the first time it had been witnessed.

"Wake up, Sam. Holy shit, wake up!"

Samuel's eyelids squeezed tighter as he grabbed the dishevelled sheet underneath him and balled the fabric up tightly in his fists.

"Holy Christ, Samuel, snap out of it. You are scaring me."

Faye leaned over his contorted body. His mouth was clasped tightly shut, fighting the demons of his mind. Attempting to wake him, she shook his shoulders with force, trying to get his eyes to open.

Taking a large gulp of air, Samuel bolted upright. The white of his eyes stared into the empty void of the room, sweat dripping down the side of his brow. Sitting back on her heels on the edge of the bed, Faye pulled her white t-shirt down to cover her knees and wiped her eyes with her hand.

"Oh, thank God you're awake. You frightened the life out of me." Using her damp, quivering hand, she wiped away the moisture from his skin as she spoke. Moving his head away from her touch, Samuel threw off the sheet that was barely covering him.

His feet hit the ground with a thud on the wooden floor. In the dawn light, Faye watched him stomp into the bathroom, slamming the door shut behind him. Her heart pounded through the light fabric loosely covering her.

Unsure what to do, she haltingly moved off the bed and towards the closed door. Stopping just short of opening it, she paused. Her fingers held the round, white handle, and holding her breath, she slowly twisted it. The sound of the key being turned in the lock startled her, making her jump away from the door in shock. In all their years together, they had never locked a door between them. There had never been a reason to. The rejection, along with Samuel's mood swings that had been occurring more often, added to the little doubts playing around in Faye's mind. After ten years together, she didn't like the way their relationship seemed to be heading and it unsettled her.

Taking a pillow from the empty bed, Faye left the man she loved behind the closed door. With the sound of the shower running, she made her way out of the room to the open plan living area. Resting the pillow at one end of the sofa, Faye lay down, pulling her knees up to her chest, and let the hurt leave the corners of her eyes, eventually falling asleep drained, confused and alone.

The sun shone into the room to welcome in the morning. Faye cursed the uncomfortable couch, stretched her tired limbs and moved cautiously towards the bedroom. Stopping at the open door, she peered inside. The bed, minus a pillow, looked no different than how she had left it in the early hours. Only then did she realise how quiet the apartment seemed. No water dripped from the shower, no toilet flushed from the bathroom. Faye looked around the room, but nothing was out of place. Samuel's clothes, taken off in a hurry last night, were hanging on the back of the chair, his sneakers still underneath the seat. Opening the small window in the room to let the day in, she stood outside the bathroom door. Leaning her ear against it, she heard nothing – no breathing, no movement. There was no one in there. When she tried the door, it opened.

The compact en-suite was masculine, with grey tiles and matching towels. Though she didn't live there, she had hoped her feminine touch would have worked in all the rooms and not just the cushions in the living area, but even her toothbrush had to be blue. Disappointed she had been left on her own, Faye quickly showered, hoping Samuel had left the apartment when she slept to bring back coffee from the café down the road, like he always did on a Saturday morning. Their time at the weekend always flew, and she hoped his absence wouldn't drag out until Sunday. After a quick shower, Faye chose an outfit from her weekend bag that matched the weather, sunny and bright, although a storm brewed inside her.

They had been inseparable friends since they'd first met each other ten years ago, and had been lovers for half of that time. Their romance had blossomed after a drunken night and a hug goodbye had become so much more. For the past three weeks, though, something had changed Samuel. A wedge had appeared between them and it was expanding at an alarming rate.

Faye could pinpoint the exact day, hour and minute when the invisible shield went up. It was midweek, and although she should have been at work, the alarm clock had failed to go off. In the mad panic of getting dressed, brushing her teeth and listening to Samuel laughing at her, the postman had arrived. Seeing Samuel's reaction as he opened the envelope, took out the A4 piece of lined paper and scanned the page had unnerved Faye. His laughter had stopped as all the colour drained from his face. Faye reached forward, resting her hand on his shirt-sleeved arm. The look he gave her, still etched in her memory, indicated that nothing would be the same again. Faye had left for work that morning with Samuel's words ringing in her ears, coldly telling her that it would be best if she only came to the apartment at the weekends. Faye had begged him to explain, told him that whatever he had just read, she was there for him, but she knew it was a waste of time. Once his stubborn attitude reared its ugly head, her words fell on deaf ears. Faye had left for work that morning and didn't return or make contact with Samuel until Friday evening, hoping that giving him a few days of space would thaw him. The letter, with its Irish stamp, was nowhere to be seen and was never mentioned, but their relationship had changed. Faye chose her words carefully when she was with him, tried to stay upbeat, but the shield Samuel had created in that one moment had remained even three weeks later.

Going into the spotlessly clean kitchen, Faye filled the kettle, took out a mug and spooned in more than the normal amount of coffee, not waiting for Samuel to return. Sitting at the breakfast counter, she flicked through the local free paper that always arrived at the weekend and went straight to the What's On section.

Saturday 10am-12pm Fun in the park ~ bring the young ones for face painting, balloon making and cake decorating.

Reaching for a pen from the chipped mug next to the phone, Faye put a line through the event. Going to a park full of families trying to control their offspring was not her idea of fun. She tried her best to avoid anywhere that had gatherings of ankle biters. The thought made her shiver. While most of her friends were settled or near settling down with their babies, Faye had no intention of using her womb for anything other than her monthlies. If she could put a stop to them, she would. Looking back down at the timetable, she also crossed out the coffee with knitting, even though you *could learn to make a scarf in a relaxed atmosphere.*

Faye held the pen over the 3pm-5pm ballroom dancing. She had gone to tap and ballet lessons back in her youth and tried to think of one good reason why she shouldn't go again. *Grab your dancing shoes and tango. Beginners welcome*, it stated. Drawing a ring around it, Faye folded the paper over with the marked event showing and left it on the counter while she went back to the boiled kettle and poured the hot water, inhaling the dark roast aroma as she did.

Checking the time on her watch, she realised an hour had passed since she woke and there was still no sign of Samuel. Thinking that maybe he'd stayed in the café to gather his thoughts, she took a yellow note from the stack of post-it notes and scribbled a short memo on it.

Gone for breakfast. Hope to see you there. x.

Rinsing the mug, Faye left it on the folded tea towel to dry, propped the note up against the kettle and left the cold feeling in the apartment behind.

At nearly nine-thirty in the morning, the streets were unusually busy with young children, probably heading to the face painting Faye had read about in the paper. Straight away, Faye regretted leaving the confines of the apartment. Keeping her head down, she darted around two slow moving children, swearing under her breath when she nearly slipped off the pavement. She just wanted to get to the little café she enjoyed most weekends with Samuel.

The rain that had fallen steadily during the week had finally cleared so the few tables on the pavement were full, leaving the café inside empty. Kelly, with her red face and countertop fan whirling around at top speed, greeted Faye as she entered and handed her a menu.

"You know I don't need one of those. Just the usual please," Faye told her, kindly refusing the menu.

"For one or two?" Kelly asked, taking a coffee mug that matched the décor from a shelf.

"Is Samuel not here?" Faye asked, looking around the empty café.

"Did you lose him?" Kelly smiled.

"I'm sure he won't be long," Faye answered as she walked to the back and sat at a table for two, not waiting to explain.

Buttering her last piece of homemade brown bread, Faye paused midway when she heard Samuel grunt something to Kelly as he entered. Biting down on the slice, she began to chew, raising her eyes to watch him pull out the chair opposite her.

"Did you order a coffee?" she asked, wanting to sound light-hearted so as not to spoil their weekend.

Samuel rubbed his unshaven chin before settling his hand on the back of his neck. Bending his head to look at the table, he shook it slightly before talking. Faye had to stop chewing to hear him, and then she had to ask him to repeat himself before she dropped the toast onto her plate and her heart nearly burst out of her chest.

"I need to see Angie in Ireland," he muttered.

"Angie? Who is Angie?" Faye leaned forward to avoid being overheard. Her favourite café was fast becoming her nightmare. She had never put his moods down to another woman, not her Samuel.

Samuel lifted his head, the dark curls still damp from a shower he must have had after she left, and pain lining his eyes.

"The woman who gave birth to me," he spat out, pushing back his chair. The noise echoed in the café, and before Faye could ask another question, he left.

Two

Stepping off the green-striped plane and down the steps onto the black tarmac, Samuel took in the vaguely familiar surroundings. The airport had grown in size from when he had last passed through it, but that was thirteen years ago and he had boxed that memory, with many more, the day he left behind the green landscape.

The day was still bright but damp from the lightly falling rain and he breathed in the odour of slurry being spread on some nearby fields and coughed.

"City folk... You need that fresh smell deep in your chest to clear any fumes you have been living in," an elderly man walking in step with him said under his breath.

"Nothing like a bit of light rain for spreading. At least the crops will benefit from all that natural fertiliser." Samuel raised his voice enough for the gentleman to know he had heard him, dismissing the city folk remark.

The passengers leaving the plane slowed, making it increasing difficult for Samuel to up his pace.

"Ah, do I hear a faint Irish accent?" the man asked when he reached him again.

"Faint it is," Samuel remarked, scuffing his size eleven feet forward.

"Home for a few days, lad?"

"Something like that."

"A man of few words. My guess is you have been away too long." Looking up at Samuel, the stranger smiled.

Samuel threw his holdall over his right shoulder while the queue that had formed came to a stop.

In front of the line stood a Garda behind a small upright desk, glasses perched at the end of his nose. Every now and then he would look over the top of them from a passport to the person and down again, before letting them through.

"Honestly, old man, I haven't been gone long enough," he said abruptly, staring ahead and waiting for his cue. Stepping forward without waiting to hear the huff the man let out, he showed his passport to the bored looking Garda and walked through the arrival doors.

One of the biggest disadvantages to travelling to the countryside was the lack of public transport. The airport had no nearby train station or bus depot, and Samuel had not checked to see what time a bus would pass, if any did. He had booked a hire car while he waited at the airport. The last thing he wanted after the morning he'd had, was to be confined in a car with someone asking questions.

That would come later.

The woman at the car hire kiosk strummed her long, painted fingernails on the plastic desk that guarded her from approaching clients. She tried to explain to Samuel that he really should have booked further in advance to get a better deal. Samuel stood mutely, waiting for her to exhaust her advice so he could get the keys, his thoughts back in the café where he had left Faye.

He hadn't been sure, until that morning, whether he would ever stand on Irish soil again, but something had snapped in him. He had to leave, and not even the tears welling up in her eyes could make him stay.

Losing patience, Samuel cleared his throat, making the woman whose nametag read 'Sheila' stop talking.

"I'm in a hurry. The wake I am over for is happening in..." Lifting his wrist up, he read the face of his watch, a present from Faye to celebrate his thirtieth birthday three years ago, "...in two hours. I'd hate to be late." His eyebrows furrowed.

"Oh, you don't want to be late for that. One moment and I'll take you to your vehicle." Sheila gulped, her expression changed and frown lines formed. Leaving her seat, she straightened her tight, royal blue skirt and gestured for Samuel to follow her.

The *Ford Mondeo* wasn't his type of vehicle. For a start, it had four wheels, not two, and whatever the hire company used to clean the interior smelt worse than the fresh silage he'd inhaled when leaving the plane. However, he had transport – boring, silver and diesel, all necessary to fit in and look like any other tourist going through the small towns.

The drive took over an hour. Samuel had calculated that it would take forty minutes, but he hadn't factored in the new bypass and missed his turn off, forcing himself to double back, much to his annoyance.

As he got closer to the fishing village, the road began to wind and his chest tightened. Pressing the button on the door, he watched the driver's window shut, closing him away from anyone he might recognise.

When he'd left ShanInis, the boom began to happen. The vast fields had been dotted with white plaques for planning permission, and cars were updated quicker than the loans could be paid. More money in the town came hand in hand with greed. Houses were built to outdo the size of the last, and the usually large Irish families were reduced down to the average two point four children, many with au pairs left to bring up the offspring, while both parents worked to support their lifestyle.

Slowing down as he reached the town, he wasn't surprised by how busy the place seemed to be late in the afternoon. The wide pavements were three deep with people stopping to look in the craft shop windows or at restaurants that had changed names since he was last there. He crawled through the main street in the hire car, his dark shades now covering his eyes in the slowly changing light. Absent-mindedly, a tourist walked off the path and onto the road, making Samuel curse and slam on his brakes, thinning his patience even more. Through the windscreen, he watched the man mouthing apologies and holding his arms out towards the car. Shaking his head, Samuel put the car into first gear and waited for the apologetic man to move, wishing he would hurry up.

He made it through the town without seeing anyone he recognised – not even a glimmer worthy of a second look at a face he may have known. He'd spent hours in the gym and changed from a boy to a man when he'd first left Ireland, but now he ran only on the days he could. The people from his past might have changed, too, but somehow he doubted it, especially if they'd stayed in that small town. But this wasn't a social visit; he didn't need the distraction, nor welcome it.

The house he needed to get to meant passing The Huddle on the edge of town. The popular drinking haunt had been the hub of ShanInis back in the day. Although not in the town, it held prime position over the other forty-five local pubs due to the lock-ins after hours and the sneaky drinks that passed through the back door for the local lads just under the age limit. To Samuel, it all seemed like a lifetime ago. The old regulars, he guessed, had either moved out of the area, were home with their families or died.

He had discovered, when he still read the local papers, that one of his old buddies had not made it out of his teens. The year Samuel left his neighbour's son, John, had taken his own life. The search had gone on for three days. Everyone had gone looking when he failed to show up at University that October. On the fourth day, his father walked into the old cowshed belonging to the farmer two fields away and found him on the end of a rope. Later, it became known that he couldn't cope with the University course he had taken. He was only nineteen.

It sickened him how dark and gloomy the place could be when the winter nights fell and the tourists left, taking their fat wallets with them. He knew that if he hadn't left, he would have ended up with the same fate.

He could see lights glowing in the pub in the distance, even though the sun had yet to set. Their shimmer had once attracted swarms of midges that flickered under the beams. In his youth, he had sat beneath those lights at night many times, squishing as many of the insects as he could between his fingers. He'd often wondered what a professional therapist would make of it. Would they have told him it was his way of relieving the pressures of home and his past? Only he knew that was only part of the tension he carried with him.

Considering the town had grown in size, it surprised him that The Huddle looked the same. The whitewashed walls and black trimmings stood out from the green fields behind. The concrete driveway extended all around the pub, which prided itself on possessing the *best beer garden in town*. Samuel had never understood why they had a beer garden in Ireland, with its damp, cold weather.

His gut started to twist with the memory of that garden – the lazy days he was supposed to be at school but instead climbed the wall at the back and wasted hours lying on the grass with Molly O'Brien by his side. She always brought a rug with her, even when it was wet. On those days, they'd huddled under the trees wrapped in the tartan. He didn't want to just lie there with her, though. He wanted to do so much more, but when his hand travelled further south, she slapped it away and giggled. Her youth and naivety told him to leave well alone. Her upbringing told him she shouldn't be with him, but one night she'd allowed him to go further, taking away both of their virginities in a fumbled moment.

He loved her for that. He was sure that a girl like Molly wouldn't still be living in ShanInis. Her parents, who owned the pub, had invested a small fortune into her future that it shocked him to know that parents would do that for their child. A fund had been set up on the day of her birth to cater for her education, and the last he knew of Molly O'Brien, she'd headed to the big city of Dublin. Since she was three years younger than him, he only could wish her well. He had moved on. Molly had to grow up and he knew keeping in touch after he boarded the train would only hold her back. He hadn't been in a good place then. He was hardly in a good place now.

He slowed the car. Outside the double fronted building, the benches were filled with early evening dwellers. Samuel opened his window an inch, and laughter and chatter entered the vehicle. With his shades trying to hide his identity, he scanned the crowd to see if any of his ghosts were there. There had only been two people he ever really hung around with – Molly being one and his old buddy Carl being the other – so he knew the chances were very slim. It was the other arseholes he tolerated during his school years that he'd rather not bump into. No amount of years could wipe away the fights he had with them after the names they'd called his family. He wouldn't trust his fists if he met them now.

It wasn't whiskey from The Huddle he had a taste for right then, but the one that sat high on the shelf in the house he was headed towards. Tonight, he needed to drink; tomorrow, he would deal with the letter stuffed into his holdall, and the shit would hit the fan.

With a bit of the Irish luck that seemed to have passed him by throughout his youth, he hoped that by the time he got back on the plane, the job he'd come over to do would be done, and the past would stay buried forever.

Pressing his foot on the gas, he sped up, leaving behind the sandy dust that the wind always brought in from the cold Atlantic sea.

Three

Closing the door of the rental broke the stillness of the country lane. Green fields reached out for what looked like miles, but in reality was only as far as the crest, which darkened the hill where the sun had started to set. Samuel had forgotten how much darker it was away from the town and its street lights. To his left stood the small, whitewashed cottage, with its grey slate roof. The small, picture box dwelling had once belonged to his uncle, who was unmarried and had manned the farm when it was thriving.

Samuel shuddered, remembering the phone call he'd received a few years ago about his Uncle Seamus. A disease had taken the animals from him, along with his pride. The darkness that had consumed him took his breath the day he swung from the rafters. He'd liked his Uncle Seamus. He was an innocent soul who had devoted his life to his animals. Samuel had been devastated he couldn't make the funeral the next day. He wasn't ready to return, so he took his anger out on the punching bag in the gym, vowing to cut down every rafter and beam to stop another life from being wasted.

From where he stood, Samuel could see the garden surrounding the cottage. It looked unkempt, and he wondered who now owned the premises and left it so unmanaged and unloved.

However, that wasn't why he'd jumped on a plane and made the journey from his safe haven to the place that had caused all his negative thoughts for many years, and more recently, the night terrors. He didn't want to be here. He didn't belong here, and he hated the way Faye had looked at him when he left. He didn't like the way she looked at him when he woke from his reoccurring nightmare, but he couldn't explain why he had to leave her. If he had then, he would have had to tell her about Angie, about the house he'd lived in and about the past he had tried for so long to forget. Faye wouldn't like the truth, and her look of pity would only break him. Now, standing in the quiet of his surroundings, he knew she could never know. That was why he was here. To end it once and for all.

Angie and his past needed to be buried.

The door of the dormer bungalow he had parked outside opened.

"Hey, I thought I heard a car." A young woman in her mid-twenties with hair as long as a horsetail stood before him.

"Dee? God, it's great to see you. It's been too long."
Samuel pulled his holdall from the back seat and pressed
the key fob to lock the doors.

"Must be two years or more since I visited ye. Way too
long. Ye know you don't have to lock the car. You're not in
the city now." Dee laughed, waving her arm to coax him
into the house. "No one is going to steal your car. Come on
before the midges eat me alive. Plus, there is a chill tonight
and I'm letting out the heat."

Samuel walked with long strides and threw his bag
over his shoulder, dishevelling his shirt in the process.

"Aren't you the bossy one? Nothing changed here
then." He smirked and leaned down to kiss the top of her
head.

"Get your arse inside, Sam. Don't want the neighbours
thinking I got a lad in to keep me company."

"What fecking neighbours?"

"I swear the Murphys at the back of the hill have
binoculars. Not normal ones but the kind that can bend
around the hill and zoom in on me," Dee replied, looking
seriously behind Samuel.

"You're talking bollocks, Dee. Why are you so
paranoid? Should I have arrived all in black, too?"

Dee closed the door behind him and shooed him into
the kitchen. Walking past Samuel, she filled up the kettle
and turned it on, gathering cups from the cupboard and
placing them on the granite worktop. Samuel watched from

the other side of the kitchen. To him, it was like walking back in time. The worktop was new, but the units were the same. Even the white goods were in the same places, although the small fridge-freezer had been replaced by an American-sized, grey monster that took over one corner where a chair had once stood. He wondered if the chair, old as it had been even back then, would be somewhere else in the house. He hoped it was.

"Not much has changed in here, Dee."

"You know what the folks are like – change nothing unless it is broken. Waste of money, Mam always said," she answered with her back to him while placing slices of cake on a plate.

"So why the change of worktop? The old one didn't break, did it?"

Turning to face him, Dee leaned against the unit, laughing. "This was only put in a few weeks ago. Told Mam to change the whole kitchen while she had the chance, but she wouldn't. Anyway, tea or coffee?"

"Coffee for now, and then I am expecting to sample some of that Irish whiskey your dad always has hidden."

"Well, ye should know where it is. You drank most of it when you lived here."

"Yeah, I bought another at the airport to replace all the stuff I drunk."

"Replace it *all*? Exactly how many bottles did ye buy?" Dee chuckled at him and continued before he could answer,

"Anyway, why don't you just open the bottle you have?"

"You must be joking. It wouldn't taste as good." He laughed and his body started to relax for the first time in several days – only a little but enough for him to take a seat and kick off his shoes.

Dee joined him at the pine table, placing two mugs of coffee on the coasters her mother insisted on using. Samuel picked his up and blew on it before tasting the bitterness. Dee watched him in the silence that had fallen over them. Since the day he'd bought a one-way ticket out of there, he hadn't been back.

The first year had been the hardest. Dee's mother's heart was broken. To Deirdre Walsh, a hardy woman, family meant everything. Working only when the kids were at school, she always had a cooked meal on the table when everyone came home. Nothing made her smile more than the sound of children playing, or when she could hear their voices travelling up the boreen from the school bus. Deirdre had hips that had birthed more than the three children who had gone full-term – two girls and a boy – but Tadgh was never meant for this world. She told everyone who dared to stop and ask that God needed him more than she did and he had greater plans for the baby. She had a wake at home, held him to her chest and rocked him for two days, his cold body wrapped in the shawl he should have been christened in. When the time came, she laid him in his white satin casket and kissed him before closing the lid on the son that took six years of praying for. Thomas Walsh, built like an ox, carried his son's casket from their home to the church, and the two girls trailed behind, holding their mother's trembling hands.

Dee put her empty mug back on the table and coughed lightly to clear her thoughts from that day, miffed that Samuel's presence in the house had brought it back. "Why did ye come now?" she asked the question that had been on the tip of her tongue since the moment he'd texted her a few hours ago.

"I need to add a full stop to something."

"Don't confuse me, Sam. I'm not letting you drink any of father's whiskey until you spill."

"That's one hell of a threat. I'll tell you what, why don't you pour me one while I go and release some water." Samuel stood up and pushed the chair back, making a scraping sound. Dee held out her hand and waved it furiously at him.

"Shush! Don't want to wake the young un."

"What young un? What the fuck are you on about?"

"There is a lot I need to tell you. You shouldn't leave it so long to get in touch."

"I do keep in touch – well, at least every six months and then there are birthdays and Christmas'."

"You have no idea when any of our birthdays are, and you never answer my calls at Christmas, so before today, I don't remember the last time you got in touch in the past two years."

"Cheers for the vote of confidence. Didn't I transfer money into your account for your twenty-fifth?"

"Yeah, so personal of you."

"I'll send a text next time and ask for the money back."

Samuel walked out of the room shaking his head. When he returned, Dee was sat at the dining table with two empty glasses waiting to be filled.

They talked into the small hours. Neither of them brought up the real reason Samuel was there or the suggestion of a child in the house. It suited Samuel just fine not to talk about it just yet. He wanted, just for a few hours, to be Samuel the man he had become not the Samuel he had been when he lived within those walls.

The whiskey bottle sat comfortably between them when they retreated to the lounge. They sat with their legs spread out on the floor and their backs to the couch. They leaned against each other increasingly the more they drunk. Dee wanted to know all about how the bar was doing and the woman in his life. He spoke with enthusiasm about The Anchor but kept talk of Faye to a minimum, not really knowing where their relationship was headed after the way he'd left her. He doubted she would still be welcoming when he returned.

As the old grandfather clock in the hallway chimed twice, he heard the front door open. Too relaxed to move, they both waited for the footsteps to reach them. They cranked their heads around to the door as it creaked open, and in the doorframe stood Deirdre Walsh. Her hair grey, she looked older than Samuel expected, and tired – very tired.

His heart pounded in his chest as he got up from the floor and embraced her.

"Now now, Samuel, it's been a long day." Deirdre pulled him from her chest. "Ye must be tired after the travelling."

It seemed like no time had passed, and Samuel felt like a teenager again. Seeing the years etched onto his aunt's face, he was humbled.

"I'm sorry it's been so long," he managed to say before hugging her again.

"How much of that whiskey have you two drunk?" Deirdre asked Dee from over Samuel's shoulder while she stroked his back comfortingly.

"Only half, Mam. Sam bought another to replace it," Dee slurred.

"Just as well. Your dad is going to need a glass when he gets back from the hospital."

"Is he still there?" Dee asked worriedly.

"He is and will be for a while yet. I've come home to see this young man. Now, Samuel, have ye eaten today?"

Samuel disengaged himself from his aunt and stood in front of her, towering over her frame by at least eight inches. He shook his head.

"Now listen here. Haven't I taught ye anything? You can't drink on an empty stomach and you certainly won't be able to face tomorrow with a sick head. Wait here and I'll check the fridge. There might be some leftovers. I'm surprised at you, Dee. Did you not offer food when Sam arrived?"

"No, Mam, we got talking and it went right out of my head. I'll help you in the kitchen." Dee began to move, but her mother put out her hand to stop her.

"No, it is fine. I'll call Samuel into the kitchen when the food is ready and then I will retire for the night. You had better get your rest, Dee. Tadgh will be awake in a few hours."

Samuel looked over to Dee, his head tilted waiting for a response to the name Tadgh, but none came forward. Instead, Dee kissed her goodnight before passing them both and leaving the room.

Deirdre Walsh was not a woman to be messed with. A straight talker to the core and known in the community as a respectable woman, she knew what they said about her behind their closed doors, but it never bothered her. Her family came first no matter what trouble they were in, and she hadn't thought twice about bringing Samuel into her home when the time came. He needed stability, and she never hesitated on the night she was approached to take him. She had heard the rumours about her sister and what was happening in that house, but who was she to intervene? How could she barge into Angela's home and take the only son she had? Plenty of times, Deirdre had taken him in for a few days while Angela was *recovering,* but the law and social services insisted Samuel stayed in his family home.

Until the day all hell broke loose. By then, though, Deirdre felt it was too late. Angela had her claws well and truly embedded into Samuel and the road to recovery was a rocky one. Although it broke her heart when he walked out and left, she knew he had to go. Now he was back, sitting at her family table eating the toasted sandwich and soup that she'd made for him, and in that brief moment, she wished she'd never posted that letter.

Four

"Faye, ring him. If I have to look at your puffy eyes for another day, I swear we will no longer be friends."

"I can't, Chloe. If you had seen the way he looked at me before he left, you wouldn't want to contact him either."

"So instead, you are going to mope around until he returns? Do you even know where he's gone?"

"Of course, I do," Faye snapped.

"Where then?"

"He said he was going to Ireland."

"Ireland? Seriously? What was the hurry? Could he not have taken you there with him for a weekend away or something?"

"I guess some things don't involve me. I think it has something to do with his mother."

"Oh, I thought she was dead." The statement hung in the air between the two friends until Faye spoke quietly.

"So did I."

Chloe reached over the breakfast counter and rested

her hand on Faye's. "And he hasn't texted at all?"

"No, not yet anyway. You know what Samuel is like, though. He is a stubborn man and when he has retreated inwards, he is best left alone."

"Yeah, but that's not a healthy relationship. You know that, don't you? He is acting like a spoilt child and needs to get his head out of his arse. You're my best friend, Faye, but he is treating you like shit."

"I know something is bugging him, stressing him out. I love him, Chloe, but this morning, the way he spoke and stared through me. It's all too much."

"Girl, I hope he is worth all the tears you have shed for him."

Faye moved to blow her nose. She had wondered the same thing herself when she'd returned home from the café alone that morning. She'd thought they were made for each other. After five years of being friends and then lovers, things had been good. He had his moments, times when he needed to clear his head or disappear on his motorbike for a couple of days, but they spoke. This time, they hadn't. For three weeks, he'd kept whatever thoughts occupied him behind tight lips. That hurt more than when he had only wanted to see her at weekends. He had always been a quiet man, but this was different. The wall he shielded himself behind had locked doors and no key.

When Faye had turned eighteen, she had been determined to enjoy her birthday in style. The new bar that had opened the previous weekend had glowing reviews. The party, consisting mostly of her friends who attended the local secondary school with her, they were happy to have a drink in their hands and a chance to dance no matter where they were. The talk spreading around the locality suggested that the barman was steaming hot, which had made the venue easy to choose. Faye entered in her tight-fitting dress and high heels. It took her walking from the door to the bar to realise the mutterings were true. All it took was the twang in his talk and the glint in his eye, and she was smitten. He was five years older than she was, and they became friends, nothing more. Faye would have dated him if he'd asked that night, but the rumours also came with talk of how he had already slept his way through the staff. That didn't sit well with her, but she talked and he listened and with no attachment, it worked.

She knew he was Irish. She wasn't that naïve. His accent had faded and become softer over time. When she questioned him about his family, Samuel had told her his mother passed away when he was seven, and the subject quickly closed after that. Only one cousin had ever visited that she could recall, but she'd only met her briefly. He was the bad boy the guys wanted to be, the girls wanted to have and adults couldn't find a reason to hate. He smoked and drank, and Faye thought he was untouchable.

When the owner of the bar decided to cash in and move abroad, Samuel declared he wanted to take over, and she'd supported him all the way. She'd even stayed up until the early hours helping with business plans and spreadsheets for meetings with the bank manager. She thought he saw her as a kid sister, never knowing he was hiding his desire for her all that time.

The bar was his project. He took to the role of manager like a duck to water and picked staff with enthusiasm. Now under his management for five years, the bar had grown and become the hub of the town.

The night he raised a toast to a packed house to celebrate his ownership, he took her into the office and seduced her. Even now, she remembered his touch along her skin and the goose bumps that had risen in anticipation. Since that night they'd become lovers, friends, and now strangers.

"Fancy going out tonight, Chloe?" Faye asked, shaking the memories from her thoughts.

"Wouldn't mind, but not all night. I'm meeting Lewis tonight and I don't want to be drunk when he arrives."

"So you are still seeing Lewis? Is it exclusive yet?"

"Well he does know how to hit the right spot, and I've been seeing him more than just at the weekends."

"Way too much information," Faye cringed as she spoke.

"You're only jealous. Haven't even texted the other guys on my list for at least two weeks now. I think I am getting all grown up."

"Well, I'm proud of you. I have no idea how you manage to see more than one guy at once anyway. It would do my head in."

"I hate to think what Samuel would do with the other guys if you did. Remember what happened when that bloke in the bar tried to hit on you? Sam turned into a caveman, all protective and stuff."

"Yeah, but if that happened now, I'm not sure he'd even see the guy?"

"Is there something you aren't telling me, Faye? Has he said or done something?"

"No, honestly, apart from disappearing to Ireland, nothing. He's been serious lately, that's all. He seems to have a lot on his mind." Throwing her tissue into the kitchen bin, Faye kept her eyes firmly on the tiled floor, taking Chloe's hands in hers.

"Let's not talk about him. Let's just go out, have a few drinks and chill." Faye gave Chloe a strained smile, looking at her from under her dark lashes.

The two girls stared at each other briefly – one wishing the other would stop asking questions to which there were no good answers.

With a broad smile, Chloe answered, "Sounds good to me, but first, I think we need some retail therapy. I need a little dress to wear tonight for Lewis to lose his hands under."

Faye laughed. "You are a terrible woman, and I am

completely jealous."

"Then buy a sexy dress yourself and show that man of yours what he is missing. You should send a picture tonight and see how long it takes for him to reply then."

Jumping off the stool, Faye slipped on her shoes and checked her purse was in her bag before switching off her phone and leaving it on the breakfast counter.

"I'm ready but forget about sending him a picture," she announced.

"You not taking your phone?"

"Nope. I told you I don't want to think about Sam at all today."

"Well, I am still taking a picture when you try on that dress. I'll send it to you and you can send it later," Chloe said while unlocking the door of Faye's apartment for them to leave.

Lewis met them in the pub after Chloe called him during their lunch. No one mentioned going to The Anchor, the bar owned by Samuel, and Faye was grateful for that. Although she loved going there, with Samuel gone, she didn't want to put on a smile for Kirk, his trusted barman, or any of the other staff. She didn't know if he had told them where he had gone and Faye was a terrible liar.

It was Saturday evening and the place was busy. After paying for their drinks, they went outside to the wooden benches and sat down near the gas heaters.

"Are you warm enough in that dress, Faye?" Lewis asked, pointing to her bare shoulders.

"I have a wrap in my bag, but it's still very mild even for September."

Turning his attention to Chloe, he draped his arm over her shoulder, drawing her closer to him. "So, did you girls have fun shopping today?"

"Do you really want to know what we bought?" Faye asked, feeling slightly awkward as the third person and hoping he didn't want to know.

"Go on, humour me."

"I'll show you what I bought later, Lew," Chloe piped up with a broad smile.

"Look forward to that, sweetheart." Leaning closer, he sealed his smile with a full kiss on Chloe's lips.

"Cut it out, you two, for fuck's sake. I don't want to be playing gooseberry here. Save it 'til later," Faye remarked, taking a slug of her drink to quench the bile rising up from her stomach.

"You are only jealous. Where is lover boy anyway? Isn't it at weekends you are allowed to stay with him?" Lewis questioned between kisses on Chloe's swollen mouth.

"Leave her alone, Lewis. She needs cheering up not depressing," Chloe scolded, wiping her mouth with the back of her hand.

"I'm sorry, Faye. What's going on?"

"If I knew I would tell you, but I don't really know anything."

"Has he ditched you to work again this evening?" he asked but didn't wait for an answer. "Seriously, if I were him and saw you in that dress, I would have you propped up at the bar where I could keep an eye on you. No way would I have other men ogling my woman, especially someone as hot as you. Look around. There are men licking their lips all over the place. See that one?"

Faye and Chloe both looked where Lewis was pointing, and there, to the left of the table, was a group of lads in their early twenties. At least three of them were eyeing Faye up. Holding on to the seam of her new dress, she tried to pull it down to cover her thighs, which were in full view, but it was pointless. The material had no stretch and clung to her skin. In that instant, she wished she'd never bought the dress. Samuel would hate it if he were here.

Lewis broke her thoughts. "Faye, he has some fucked up ways of expressing his love for you. Are you sure he is worth it?"

"I think I need another drink. Anyone else want one?" Faye's voice cracked a little, evading the question she didn't know how to answer.

By ten o'clock, Faye was in her pyjamas, her fingers hovering over the keys on the phone in her hand. She made an excuse to leave the two lovebirds after the third drink.

Chloe was her best friend, but when she was involved with a man, she had no time for anyone else, and Faye had had enough of being sociable for one night.

The keypad beckoned her to type a message, any message, to Samuel. Pressing the letters, she wrote four short words and hesitated. She knew he would be in touch on his terms only. Nothing she said would make him text her back or even call. Unless she did what Chloe suggested and send the photo of her in the new dress.

Loading the photo to send as an iMessage, she hesitated. Whatever he had to do, whatever had made him jump on a plane without any explanation, it had to be serious, and right now, she was being selfish. This was not how a normal relationship should be, no matter how much she loved being with him.

Switching off her phone again, Faye laid her head back on her pillow and waited for sleep to take her through her tears.

Five

Samuel woke in the small spare room to an eerie silence. The walls had changed from the pale pink paint that once covered them to a neutral off-white. This had once been Dee's room, the compact domain she'd spent many hours in. By default, the box room, as it was called, was given to the youngest until another room became vacant. When Samuel lived there, he spent hours in his bed listening to his cousin's feet running up and down the stairs or the shouting between siblings. The house was always a hive of activity, with extra help from the farm during lambing season or preparing the fields for bailing. The farmhouse was a busy one. Now, though, he could hear nothing but his breath.

He checked his phone for the time and noticed that none of the text messages he had yet to answer were from Faye. Switching it off, Samuel lay back on the cream pillow and closed his eyes. For a woman, he thought loved him despite all his faults, the strain of keeping her at a distance for the past three weeks may have taken its toll.

Faye was the first girl he'd loved since Molly O'Brien, if you could call what they had at such a young age love. He'd had enough lovers before Faye to fill a headboard with notches, but the desire to care for someone, to want no other stopped at Faye. Samuel had no idea where they were heading. Marriage never entered his head, but he knew or at least thought he knew before yesterday, they would be together for years to come.

Just thinking about her made his cock twitch. Lying in the single bed reverted him back to his teenage years, and the one thing that offered relief and helped him to forget about his youth – forget about the doubts and concentrate on the woman he'd left in the café – was the string. Not just any piece of string but the one he took the day all hell broke loose in his mother's house and he was whipped away from the torment he'd lived in. Unconsciously, he had packed it in his holdall before he left.

Reaching for his bag, he took the worn threads entwined together, frayed and grey, from the inside pocket. He began to thread it between his fingers, spreading his digits wide. Relaxing back against his pillow, he closed his eyes and relaxed into the sensation, tightening it with each twist and allowing his body to respond. The previous day's travels started to melt from his memory as the blood rushed around his body, the light bed cover he'd placed over himself tented. After the last turn, he bent his finger over, tightening it, and lost his free hand between his legs. Slowly, he eased the building pressure by stroking his cock, letting out a soft groan.

A knock on the door made him jolt upright and he swore under his breath, removing his hand quickly from beneath the cover. He quickly pulled the piece of string from his finger, leaving behind small red dents in a crisscross pattern. He swore again while he hid the worn out threads beneath the sheet.

"What?" he shouted at the door, slightly out of breath.

"It's only me. Can I come in?" Dee whispered through the panelled wood.

Samuel puffed up the blanket to hide the evidence of his deflating cock and then brushed back his hair with his fingers, confident that his breathing sounded normal again.

"Yeah, come in."

The round doorknob turned with a click before the door opened. Dee peered around the edge, slowly entering.

"Are ye decent?"

"Come in, Dee," he answered.

She entered further into the room, her left hand covering her eyes, and closed the door behind her.

"Last time I entered your bedroom, you were semi-naked. Tell me now, Samuel, are you really decent?"

"Fuck sake, woman," he said chuckling at her attempt to reach the bed without falling. "Take your hand away from your eyes. I'm decent, I tell you."

48

Spreading her fingers, Dee peeked through the gaps, removing her hand once she had confirmed it was safe.

"Thank feck for that. I know we are kinda like siblings, but some things don't need to be shared."

"God, you are daft. Anyway, I wasn't semi-naked the last time. I was wearing boxers."

"Blue ones, if I recall. The memory has been etched in my brain for years now."

"Dee, just sit down," he instructed, patting the spot beside him on the bed.

She sat down cautiously where he suggested, wearing a grey tracksuit that nearly matched the bed cover. Samuel wondered if she had been out for a run but she didn't look flushed, her feet were bare and her hair had yet to see a brush. Resting her leg on the bed to face him, Dee rubbed the yellow band on her finger.

"Still wearing it then?" Samuel asked, pointing at the index finger on her left hand.

"Habit really. One day I'll take it off."

"No man will look at you if you stay attached to it."

"You would be surprised, Sam. Sometimes a ring attracts men, even if it's just for one night."

"So, is this the part where you tell me about the child you mentioned last night?"

"It is. I wanted to tell you before he woke, which won't be long now."

"You know whatever happened I'll support you."

"No need for that. You have supported Mam long enough. The last thing you need is someone else's mistakes to sort out."

Reaching over, he rubbed the back of her hand gently. "I'm here for you, girl – you and the child. Never doubt that."

"I can't believe I kept him from you, but he isn't my secret to tell and I didn't want to be a disappointment. Then Mam sent the letter. If you had rung or got in touch, I would have said, but you didn't. Yesterday I was making bottles and then out of the blue, you texted. That came as a shock. I told Mam you wouldn't come all that time we heard nothing, but she just said, *God is good*, like she always does. I'm sorry. I really am sorry." Dee took in a needed breath and wiped her eyes with the back of her hand, keeping her head bent to look at the floor.

"Hey, no need for tears. Life happens and I'm a stubborn arsehole. So what if you made a bad call? Look what you received from it – a baby. Isn't that amazing? You had a baby."

As she moved her hand away from her face, Samuel watched Dee straighten her shoulders before her eyes darted between his.

"Samuel, the baby isn't mine."

"Oh, he isn't?" Samuel's forehead crinkled. "I don't understand. Didn't you say there was a baby, a boy?"

"Yes, but *I* didn't have a baby."

"Then who does Tadgh belong to?"

"He isn't mine. I didn't give birth to him."

Shaking his head, he removed his hand from hers, leaving them folded on his lap.

"Start at the beginning, Dee, because it is too early in the morning to confuse me without coffee."

Taking a deep breath, Dee played with her ring again, looking down at the pattern while talking.

"Tadgh belongs to Millie, but she is working in America so, me and Mam are looking after him. Mam said it was better this way or it meant Millie had to give up her plans."

"Millie? As in Millie your eldest sister Millie? Perfect, can do no wrong, not married Millie? The Millie that looked down on the family and moved Stateside so she could live the high life?" Samuel asked, his voice rising with each question.

"Yes, Samuel, that Millie."

"Well, fuck me. I didn't expect that. But why all the secrecy? It's not the 70's."

"Millie wanted to give him up for adoption. Mam wouldn't hear of it, so they came to an arrangement. We bring him up and Millie can carry on with her career."

"And what about your plans? Deirdre isn't able to mind a baby and do all the other things she has on at the moment."

"I have no plans. Look at me. I'm a twenty-five-year-old who lost her fiancé to the devil. I have no life left."

"You need to get away from this town, Dee. You need to move away and start again. You. Are. Young. You. Are. Beautiful. Come back with me and I will give you a job to start you off."

"Stop with that talk right now, will ye? It is no good to me and certainly no good to Tadgh or Mammy. I just wanted to let you know about him so you don't stress Mam out with questions. She is too exhausted to argue with you."

Samuel unfolded his arms, the hair standing up on the back of them in his anger. He knew she was right. He would question and that would end up in an argument. He wasn't here for that and needed to conserve his energy for the real reason for his return. Letting out a breath that was building into steam, he leaned towards her.

"Tell me something, Dee. What the fuck has been going on here? And why the hell haven't I been told about any of it?" He wanted to stomp across the room to open a window and let in some air, and it frustrated him that he couldn't in his boxers and t-shirt.

"Don't be cross. You have no right to be. When you walked out of that door, your last words nearly broke Mam's heart."

"Fuck, I was mad back then. I was a stick of dynamite ready to explode."

"Yeah, well Mam thought it was best to only drip feed you the news from here. She was scared you would end up in prison or disappear like your Da. "

"He's no Father of mine. He's a fucking waste of fresh air. I wouldn't even call him my sperm donor. Wherever or whoever he is, I'm sure he never looked back the day he left."

"Don't say that. He is your flesh and blood."

"That man should have been put down at birth. Not one ounce of goodness came from him."

"Ye did."

"I don't know about that, Dee. I really don't know if we are that different. It's not like I ever met him to compare."

"But you have seen pictures, haven't you?"

"No, nothing, only what Angie drummed into me from the moment I could hear."

"She had her own problems."

"She sure did and I was one of them."

"And at the end of that downpour, the sun shone and you became kind of my brother, so that's enough of that talk."

"S'pose. I tell you one thing – it's a pity that arsehole of a Father doesn't have a name so I could trace him down. I would love to have a chat involving my fist."

"You really have no clue at all of what he looks like?"

"I didn't exactly go looking for information when I lived in that hell hole. I was too busy staying out of the way."

"Sorry, Samuel, I didn't..."

"It's fine, but thinking about it makes my blood boil."

"Look, I'll leave ye to get ready. You have a big day today. I'll put on the kettle downstairs."

"Thanks, Dee. You know this conversation isn't over, though?" Samuel leaned forward, kissed Dee on the forehead and then ruffled her hair like he had done when she was a kid.

"It is, for now, Sam. It is for now."

After showering, he dressed in his dark jeans and crisp, white shirt and put on his loafers. Downstairs in the kitchen, he poured his coffee from the percolator Dee had prepared and then went out to the back garden. The sun had risen and the air felt warm for the middle of September. The fence around the courtyard looked worn and in desperate need of a lick of paint. If he'd had more time, Samuel would have got to work. He had always been an outdoor kid when he'd lived here, working on the land every moment he had, and he would have liked nothing better than to roll up his sleeves and do the work. However, this wasn't his home anymore and he felt sure the only reason the fence lacked paint was the family's current time constraints. Although this was his first visit back to his home country in thirteen years, he felt no guilt. He wondered if his life would have turned out differently if he had stayed, but he knew the answer to that.

He probably would have been dead.

Six

Dee stood in the kitchen washing bottles at the Belfast sink. He knew from where she was standing she could watch him outside and he was grateful she didn't join him out there. After finishing his coffee, looking out to the fields, he ventured back in to find Dee still in her tracksuit and grey hoodie. Her dark near black hair tied up into a messy ponytail.

"So, what's happening today? Are ye heading into town?"

"My return ticket is for tomorrow. I don't really have time to be touring around."

Samuel leaned against the granite worktop and crossed his legs at his ankles, the empty mug keeping his hands busy.

"You look very at home there. Looking after Tadgh seems to suit you," he remarked.

"If you're being sarcastic then don't bother. I know what I look like and radiant is not it." Dee rolled up the sleeve of her sweater with her wet hand and blew a stray hair out of her eyes.

"There is definitely a man out there missing a great wife," Samuel commented, hoping not to offend her.

"There *was* a man out there, Sam. You know that. Now I am happy to have only Tadgh in my life. At least I have some control over him."

"Have you spoken to anyone since...well you know, since that day?" he asked quietly. Her washing up picked up speed, the water splashing onto the floor making Dee swear and then bless herself afterwards. Holding onto the sink, she paused and her shoulders sunk. Samuel opened his mouth, but before he could say something, anything to reverse what he had said, the washing up continued.

"A doctor, you mean? What's the point? Like Mam would say, put your big girl knickers on and get on with life. Ye know what this town is like – gossip or be gossiped about. I'm getting there, Sam. You of all people should know it doesn't just take a few years to move on." She blurted the words out so quickly that he realised she must have rehearsed those lines a few times over the years. "I still miss him."

"You're only twenty-five, Dee. You have years ahead of you. I still think you need to move from here," he stated bravely. "You need a change of scenery, a fresh start."

"We are not talking about this again, Samuel Delaney. You're not here to sort out my life. Remember that." Dee kept her back to him, but he watched her body tense as she spoke. She was right. He wasn't there to sort out her life. He didn't even want to sort out his own.

Without another word, Samuel placed his mug on the counter behind him and walked out of the room, retrieved his keys from the hallway and left the house through the front door.

Samuel sat in the hire car for a few minutes, his hands clenched around the leather steering wheel while he waited for his temper to settle. It annoyed him to see his cousin still living at home and now looking after her sister's child. He doubted she would ever leave the area and he couldn't tell her that, not in those words anyway. Anytime Dee visited him, she loved the vibrant life he lived, the bar he owned and the culture that surrounded her. She nearly took the plunge. When she was twenty and engaged to her teenage sweetheart, she'd had plans.

After leaving school, Dee had secured a University place in the same area as Owen, her fiancé. He had been in his final year when Dee began her degree in business. Samuel had teased her, telling her to hurry up and finish so he could hire her to tidy up his paperwork and sort out his office. Two years into her degree, the year he passed the bar for his law degree, Owen became sick. The phone call Samuel had received from his aunt still haunted him.

It was aggressive. He never knew. He didn't have long.

Just thinking about it had bile rising into Samuel's mouth. He opened the door and spat onto the gravel. Wiping his mouth with the back of his hand, he covered his eyes with his dark shades and leaned back in the seat. He wanted more for his cousin. She deserved that after Owen's death, another funeral he hadn't attended. He hated the idea of visiting a councillor but thought Dee needed to. Maybe a professional could show her the light she seemed to have lost.

The sun was shining, making the fields look a lighter shade of green. How many times had he run through them for what he'd thought was miles when he was a kid?

The school holidays had felt like they went on forever. Most days he'd helped Uncle Seamus and the crew of men making haystacks or preparing the land for growing potatoes and other vegetables, one of the many ways his uncle made a bit of cash. Today wasn't a day for memories, though, so Samuel got back out of the car, shut the door and locked it.

The small path that led to his uncle's cottage was overgrown, but he knew the route even with his eyes closed. Reaching the small rusty gate, Samuel swung it back and forth on its hinges to free it enough to squeeze through the gap. He brushed off the flecks of rust that clung to his jeans, then rolled up his sleeves and opened the top two buttons of his shirt.

Rubbing the bristles on his chin, he started the climb

down the twelve overgrown steps to the foot of the garden. At the bottom, he stood with his hands on his hips, looking down past the jungle before him to the cottage. There was a clearing with dry grass flattened to make a pathway around to the front of the bungalow. The farm dogs had used it as a shortcut to run from field to field and created their own path over the years, treading down the grass with their padded feet.

Samuel took their route, cutting across the flat grass to reach the brown back door. The door was locked, not even budging when he used his shoulder against it. Samuel turned his attention to the window beside it. The catch on the old timber was loose, and when Samuel pushed it, it opened a little. He looked through the gap and saw the door had a bolt across it, keeping it shut. Leaving the window to close again, he trampled around to the front of the cottage and onto the concrete path, being careful not to blindly walk into any drains. Once he had reached the front door, which was identical to the back – brown and worn through lack of paint – he tried the handle but it, too, was firmly locked. Giving up on the idea of entering, he took a step back to view the rest of the cottage. It looked worn, tired and unloved.

He sat down on the front doorstep and pulled out one of the packets of cigarettes he'd picked up from duty-free. He wasn't really a smoker, not for a long time, but coming back, he needed one of the vices he'd enjoyed when he lived here, that and the faithful piece of string in his bag.

Holding the stick between his lips, he lit a match from the box he'd found in the lounge last night, and ignited the end. Taking in a deep breath, he closed his eyes, leaned back against the door and smoked his first cigarette in six years. The burn down his throat felt good. With each inhale, he dragged it deep into his lungs before expelling it out into the country air.

Poison mixed with fresh air.

His life mixed with Faye's.

He lit another off the end of the first as the heat of the late summer sun beat down on him. He heard his name being called in the distance, so stubbing out his cigarette, he got up and stretched. Tucking his dishevelled shirt back into his jeans, he walked around to the back of the cottage.

"Hey, I have been looking for you. What ye doing down there?" Dee shouted, holding a wriggling baby on her hip.

"Just wanted to have a look around. Do you have a key to the place?" Samuel asked, re-tracing where he had walked earlier.

"Mam does, but no one has been in there for a while. It's probably overrun with rats by now."

Samuel reached the bottom of the steps and shielded his eyes with his hand, even though he had his sunglasses on.

"So this is baby Tadgh then?"

"Yeah, this is him. Don't let these cute cheeks fool you," Dee answered, squeezing the little boy's cheeks as she spoke.

Samuel smiled, listening to the gurgling chuckle coming from the tot.

"He likes you."

"And so he should. I'm his Aunty Dee and my job is to spoil him."

"Well don't spoil him too much."

"That will never happen. He is going to grow up to be a strong Walsh boy and help out on the farm."

"Or not," Samuel remarked, raising his eyebrow.

"Close your ears and don't listen to that man, Tadgh. You'll stay here with Aunty Dee, won't you?"

Samuel shook his head. This wasn't his battle to fight. He would leave that to Tadgh when he got older.

"If Deirdre has a key, I might ask if I could have a nose inside," he said, going back to the subject of the old cottage.

"Samuel, there is nothing but Uncle Seamus's old furniture stored in there. The place needs pulling down if you ask me." Dee swapped the baby to her other hip, changing footing at the same time.

"What did you want me for, Dee?"

"Oh, Mam wants you. She is waiting in the lounge."

"Oh dear. If your mother is sitting down in the middle of the morning, it must be serious."

"Ye should have come back sooner, Sam."

"Well I am here now," Samuel replied, walking up the steps to the open gate to follow Dee who had already started her walk back.

Seven

Dee busied herself in the kitchen, leaving Tadgh to play on a mat on the floor. She prepared a teapot and refreshed the coffee machine. The tray already held a plate of Kimberly biscuits, homemade fruitcake and a teacup for her mother. Her hands shook a little when she poured the boiling water into the pot. She knew that when her mother ordered her to get a tea tray ready and waited in what they called the posh lounge, it was serious. She just hoped whatever her mother had to confront Samuel with wouldn't have him running back to the UK and not returning for another thirteen years.

He was her favourite cousin, the only one on her mother's side of the family. She'd admired him right through her youth. Her friends had always wanted to get a sneak peek at him when he was baling hay in the summer with his shirt off, and he'd given her the strength to continue after losing Owen. She never told him any of that, but she hoped that deep down he knew.

Dee knocked on the door of the *posh lounge* before opening it. Holding the tray steady, she placed it down on the coffee table in front of Deirdre Walsh and backed out. It wasn't until she closed the door that she could breathe again.

Deirdre sat tight-lipped and stirred the bag in the teapot before pouring it and adding a dash of milk to her teacup. Samuel watched every move she made from by the window where he stood.

"Take your coffee, Samuel. I am sure it's not the same as you drink in the city but this is only a humble home and we only have an old coffee machine."

"It tasted lovely earlier and I am sure it will taste just as good now." Samuel moved towards the table, now that his aunt had broken the silence, and picked up his mug.

"There is milk, too," Deirdre stated, pointing to the small white jug on the tray.

"Thank you, but I like mine black. It suits me," Samuel answered.

"Sit down, Samuel. You're making the room look untidy," Deirdre ordered, nodding towards the settee opposite her.

He smiled. The woman before him had lived a hard life and yet she still made him feel like a teenager and not quite a man.

"You got the letter?" she asked, looking directly at him while drinking her tea.

"Yes. I wouldn't be here if I hadn't."

"I'm disappointed in you."

"You are? Why? Haven't I made good for myself since I left?" he asked, resting his elbow on the arm of the chair and crossing his legs.

"It has been thirteen years. Thirteen years ago you walked out of here and never came back. I mention *Angela* in one letter, out of all I have sent you, and you're suddenly here in my house. How do you think that makes me feel?"

Samuel stayed silent. She was completely right, but he couldn't think of an answer to give her. His life had been different since the envelope arrived through his letterbox. That was why he'd jumped on the plane, why he was sitting here, facing the rage of his aunt. She must have been holding what she wanted to say to him back last night.

"I took ye in when you had nowhere to go. Do you remember that? Has that slipped your mind since the bright lights of the mainland have been blinding ye? Well has it?"

Placing his half empty mug back onto the tray, Samuel sat forward in his seat, resting his elbows on his knees, his chin on his hands, and looked at his aunt.

"I haven't forgotten what you have done for me. That is why I set up the direct debit to you each month. I wouldn't be who I am today if it weren't for what this family did for me back then." He spoke slower and calmer than his aunt to make what he said clear.

"Well, you sure have a funny way of showing it."

"You could have visited me. I did offer to book you a flight several times."

"What and get on a metal thing that flies up in the sky? I don't think so. If God wanted me to fly, he would have given me wings, not legs."

"Then we are both at fault," Samuel said, barely audibly.

Deirdre sipped her tea through tight lips, and Samuel was grateful for the respite to get his head around his aunt's outburst. Strangely, he hadn't thought she would be upset about him coming back but happy to see him. Last night's reunion had given him false hope, regardless of what got him there.

Samuel rubbed the back of his neck with the palm of his cool hand. The room felt stuffy all of a sudden, his shirt starting to stick to his body. He needed air but knew he couldn't leave the room after Deirdre had ordered him there. Getting up, he opened the window, letting in a slight breeze. Breathing it down into his lungs, he waited until he heard the tea cup on the tray before returning to sit ready to face her again.

"Why did you send me the letter, Deirdre?" Samuel asked. It was what he had been thinking about a lot since the envelope had arrived.

Deirdre folded her arms across her chest. He waited for her answer, watched her lips twist to one side while she

66

thought of how to respond. She had aged over the years he had been gone, not in an old way, but her hair was duller and tied up into a bun, giving her a grandmother look. The trousers and jeans she had once worn had given way to long skirts to help hide the thickening of the hips age sometimes gave the womanly figure after fifty. He doubted she had let herself go in the fashion department, but he did think that maybe she was just too tired to bother.

Deirdre Walsh licked her dry lips and straightened her skirt. With a slight quiver in her speech, she spoke, "Ye had a right to know, Samuel."

"Did you not think that maybe I didn't want to know?" Samuel responded before her last word was out.

"You're the next of kin. Nothing can be done without your say."

"Could have let her suffer. Don't you think she deserved that?"

"Samuel Delaney!" Deirdre raised her voice, blessing herself at the same time. "Dear Jesus, if God heard ye, he would have struck you down. Holy Mary, Samuel, you're not too young to get your mouth washed out with soap and your arse smacked across my knee."

Taking a napkin off the tray, Deirdre blotted her face and then used it to wipe the back of her neck, muttering under her breath at the same time. Samuel knew she was reciting the rosary. It was something she used to do anytime she walked into his old home. And now she was doing it because of him.

Samuel waited until his aunt had calmed down. The last thing he wanted was for his Uncle Thomas to come home from the hospital or working on the land to see the state of his wife, so he topped up the small tea cup with the leftover milk and handed it to his aunt to drink.

"You need to go to the hospital. Thomas is there, but I'll call him to let him know you are on your way. This has to be sorted, Samuel – no more suffering, no more hurt, no more hidden lies," she begged, taking the cup from him and drinking all the milk in one mouthful.

Samuel knew his aunt was right. He wouldn't have jumped on a plane and been back in Ireland if he hadn't.

He left the house promising to go to the hospital, which calmed his aunt down and resulted in a much-needed Deirdre hug. The small worry lines at the sides of her brown eyes looked less tense by the time he was in his hire car.

Opening the car window as he drove, he inhaled the salt drifting in from the ocean, hoping it would wash the bitter taste from his mouth. When he got on that plane thirteen years ago, he'd thought that was the end of his troubles. Coming back here was never in his plans, but he did miss the sea and how it calmed him. He had visited the coast on the mainland a few times on his *Harley,* but seeing and hearing the Atlantic was something completely different. He had forgotten how serene the place could be and he fully understood why the area had become so popular. What they didn't know, though, was that many years ago, behind drawn curtains in the middle of the day, a young boy's life could have ended very differently. Coming back was not optional. It had to be done. He just hoped it wasn't going to be the biggest mistake he had ever made.

Samuel drove until he reached a place he used to call 'the end of Ireland'. He needed time to think, to clear his head and prepare himself.

Parking the car in the makeshift car park, he locked the vehicle, walked a few metres and stood to stare out at the vast sea. The ocean went on for miles, seemingly with no end. A young couple stood near Samuel, their backs to the sea with the railing between them and the drop down the cliff. The two of them huddled together taking pictures using the man's cell phone, laughing as they checked the results. Samuel moved away. He could have offered to take a picture for them but didn't. Walking further along the railing, he followed the path down the slope towards a hut, a new addition over the years. Entering, he pushed his shades to the top of his head and ordered a coffee at the counter. The seat he sat in overlooked the sea. From inside his jeans pocket, his phone started to vibrate.

Samuel closed his eyes and took a breath in. For an instant, he hoped it wasn't Dee asking why he hadn't reached the hospital, but she couldn't have known unless she had a tracker on him. He wouldn't have arrived yet anyway. Thinking instead that it may be Faye, his heart dipped. He couldn't speak to her yet, not until he cleared up the loose ends over here, and then he wouldn't know what to say, how to apologise, how to explain what he came here to do.

Reluctantly, he pulled out his phone. Seeing the name displayed across the screen, he answered.

"What's up, Kirk?" he asked casually of his second in command at the bar.

"Not much, boss. Got a delivery here that needs to be signed off," Kirk answered, his London accent sounding stronger in the echoes of the wooden hut.

"Why you calling then? You sign off most of the deliveries."

"But this one isn't for the bar and isn't on our order list."

"Can you see what it is?"

"Hold up, I'll just check."

Samuel could hear the phone being put down on the bar and a rustle before Kirk spoke again.

"Says here that it is from a Ms. Delaney and the stamp is from Ireland. Do you know who that is?"

"Is there a full return address?" Samuel asked.

The day after he'd moved to London, he changed his name to Walsh on all his post. Anything to dispel the connection with his mother, but he hadn't told anyone in his family that he wanted nothing more to do with the Delaney name.

"Nah, no address. What do you want me to do?"

"Just sign for it, put it in my office and I'll deal with it later."

"No worries. Are you heading in today?"

"I'm out of town. Hold the fort until I get back."

"Okay, boss. Switch off your phone. You and Faye could do with a few days for yourselves."

"Thanks, Kirk, now take your mind out of the gutter and get back to work."

Samuel finished the call and put the phone back in his pocket, not correcting Kirk on his assumption. No message had arrived from Faye. He had risked more than he realised being on Irish soil.

Samuel checked his watch. He had sat watching the waves over two mugs of coffee and the time had galloped forward. The couple he had seen earlier sat at a table not far from him, gazing at each other rather than the sea, which seemed pointless. Samuel put his mug back on the counter and paid the young girl who had served him earlier.

"Did you enjoy the view from the window?" she asked as she handed over his change.

"Yes, thank you," he replied, taking notice of her for the first time since arriving. "Are you local?"

"Not really. I'm only here during the summer months and any weekend I can persuade Mam to allow me."

"You just looked familiar."

"People say I look like my mam. Maybe you know her."

"I doubt it but thanks for the coffee."

Samuel stepped back and took in the young girl one more time before leaving the counter. Her hair was gathered in red curls on top of her head and he could only guess that it would fall down her back if it were allowed. Her eyes looked warm, and in that brief moment, he thought he could see someone he knew in them, someone never forgotten. Swallowing the lump that had formed in his throat, Samuel left the hut and rolled down his sleeves against the breeze rising from the sea, and headed back to the silver vehicle.

Eight

Not wanting to wait for the elevator, Samuel took the concrete steps two at a time and arrived at the third floor without a bead of sweat on his brow. Turning the corner, he pushed the ward door open and walked up to the nurse's station. The smell of disinfectant and stale urine clung to the inside of his nostrils and made him desperate for a cigarette.

"Can I help you?" asked a woman in a white uniform with a pleasant smile.

"Err yes, I am looking for Angie Delaney."

"Angie?"

"Sorry, I mean Angela Delaney. I was told she's on this ward, but I forgot the room number," he lied. He knew which room she was in, but the numbers on most of the doors he'd passed were missing or faded and he didn't want to enter any of them.

She asked him what relation he was, if any, and when he told her, she blinked before asking to see proof. Samuel took out his driving licence and showed her his ID. Checking the file that rested on her desk, she ran her unpolished, short nail along until she stopped by his name.

"Your name isn't exactly the same on the visitors list. The surname is different," she said, holding her finger over the list.

"No, it is my Aunt's name, Angie's blood sister. She brought me up."

"I'll have to check with the senior nurse just to make sure. Please wait here while I make a call."

Samuel watched the young nurse disappear with the portable phone. Before he could finish reading the poster explaining how to wash his hands thoroughly, she had returned.

"We expected you sooner," she remarked, walking towards him.

"I was busy."

"You do know why you are here, why we needed you here sooner, don't you?"

"Yes, but like I said, I was busy." Samuel kept his stance. He didn't feel the need to give details of his delay. He was sure the young woman before him had no idea who or what Angie really was to him.

"Follow me. She is in the special ward through the doors at the end of the corridor. Only visitors on my list can go through," she stated, cooler with him after her call.

Samuel followed her through the next set of doors and

the smell became cleaner – less urine based and more bleach. He waited for the nurse to speak to another in charge. Their whispering, for longer than he thought was necessary, started to annoy him. If they were going to discuss him, they could at least wait until he had left. They both looked up from the desk as the new nurse directed her attention to him.

"I am sure you are anxious to see your mother after your journey, Mr. Delaney. Mrs. Delaney has had the best care from the doctors in this hospital since she was admitted," the new nurse explained, lowering her voice.

Samuel's patience was slowly fading.

"I can not thank the staff enough for all their hard work. I am sure when Angie arrived all those months ago, the workload was... *difficult.* My faith is in the doctors who are treating her. I'm here to sign the papers, then this chapter can be closed and you hard working nurses can sleep soundly at night knowing you did an amazing job."

Samuel clasped his fingers together behind his back, waiting for the response he needed.

The first nurse mumbled under her breath, covering her mouth with her hand. Her eyes were wide. He met her watery gaze and strained his lips to curve up until she looked away.

"It isn't as simple as that, Mr. Delaney. I need to contact the doctor in charge and the team that cares for your mother. They would like to have a meeting with you before anything is signed. I am not sure how they do it over in England but this is Ireland and we need to follow the laws here," the second nurse told him from her seat behind the desk, clear, precise and not to be questioned.

The words were on the tip of his tongue to tell her exactly how his mother should be treated, but he decided he had said enough. The process he'd hoped would be over with his signature had started to drag on unnecessarily. Nodding to them both, he offered his forgiveness and blamed his tiredness for his directness, eager to put his name on the very important paper.

"Would it be possible to arrange a meeting to discuss the next step then?" he asked politely, stepping forward to rest his forearms on the desk.

"I will put in a call, but it is the weekend, Mr. Delaney. These things take time to organise."

"I would appreciate it if you could contact the doctor in charge. I could talk to him over the phone to explain my predicament." Samuel's mouth lifted at the edges in an attempt to smile again, noticing the nurse's eyes had started to soften towards him.

Her lips thinned, and Samuel could see a battle going on in her head over the right thing to do as she pulled her mouth to one side, thinking.

He stepped back, biding his time.

Rocking back on his heels, he waited. The stifling heat creeping up his back made his palms damp and his nape sweat. Everything about the people-infested, smelly building, made him uncomfortable.

He saw a flash of the day the authorities came crashing into his house. The old doctor with a walking stick had made him turn around several times, naked. He couldn't remember why. He didn't want to.

The room in the hidden part of his memory glowed white. A table, a chair, and a grumpy, grey-haired matron, with the one black tooth, were the only other things in the darkness. He shuddered, the memory not welcome, not now, not ever.

The first nurse crouched ear level with nurse two and muttered something he couldn't hear. Nurse two nodded, catching Samuel's glance, and lifted the portable phone from its cradle. After a few moments of silence, the phone connected and she began apologising to whoever was on the other end for calling on a Sunday afternoon, her eyes fixed on Samuel while she spoke. He knew she was pissed at him and could only guess what an earful she was getting. She continued to talk for a few more moments, stating that Mr. Delaney had arrived and explaining that his time in Ireland was limited. He hadn't said that to her, but apparently he didn't need to.

"I'll take you in to see your mother now. The team should be here in a few hours to talk to you, Mr. Delaney," the nurse explained to him.

Samuel put his hands in pockets of his jeans. The urge

to ball them into fists had his teeth grinding together behind the strain of his lips. He had mentioned already that he had no intention of seeing *her*. He'd given his visit to the hospital fifteen minutes tops, and it had already been over thirty.

The nurse moved ahead, but his feet hadn't moved an inch. The hum of machines vibrated in his ears each time one of the doors opened around him. He swallowed.

Was this his punishment for forcing her to make the phone call to the doctor on his day off, he wondered?

He willed his feet to move, to walk the same route as the nurse. At thirty-three years old, the fear of seeing his mother still made his heart race, pumping blood too fast around his body. He had to follow; he couldn't let the nurse think she had one over on him.

Making his strides long, to shorten the time it took, he reached the door where nurse two waited. Her features softened a fraction, her hand resting on the closed door of room eight.

"You might be a little shocked to see your mother this way after all this time. There is a chair beside the bed. Talk to her. Let her know you are here. She will be able to hear you, although she may not respond." She explained with a sympathetic look.

Samuel stood tall above the nurse, close enough to read the name on her badge. The typed black capitals read *ORLA*. She didn't look like an Orla, Samuel thought. She looked more like a Mary or a Breda, a name that represented her attitude and age. He didn't know how old she was, but he guessed around early fifties. Orla belonged to a younger woman, vibrant, arty, loved life and had a passion for travelling. Not someone who worked in a ward that catered for terminally ill patients had dark shadows under her eyes and a smile that was trained for sympathy. He didn't need that kind of smile. He didn't care if his mother had a tube up her arse and out of her ear.

Him being there did not mean he cared.

Him being there meant he could rid himself of a past he had no intention of mourning.

The thought of sitting with her, being in the same room as her, even though she had no speech, made his stomach turn, though, and he wasn't the kind to pretend all was well for the sake of others. Putting a foot into that room, without anyone present, would only result in one outcome.

He would pull the tubes from her and watch her die.

Slow. Undignified. Painful.

"Mr. Delaney?" Nurse Orla waited with the door open, her arm stretched out holding the handle. "In you go. I'll get someone to bring you some tea."

Her mouth curved slightly at the edges, then she let out a sigh – one that stated her patience with him was getting thin.

"You know what, I think it would be best for me to get

one of those amazing coffees from the shop, and a fruit scone with lashings of jam and butter. And I can read today's paper in peace, without being in a room that probably smells of piss, a stone cold heart, and death. The only day I want to be in that room with that woman is when I do the honours and switch off her life support. Only then will I smile a genuine smile."

Even with his hands in his pockets, he still tried to ball them up. He would have liked nothing more than to lash out, not at the nurse but a wall, something hard and solid so he could try to feel the pain because right then he felt nothing but anger.

"Oh, uh, right." Orla stumbled as she closed the door. "I guess I had better get your number for when the team arrives."

"I will jot it down at the desk on my way out. No need to guide me. I can remember the way."

Samuel left an open-mouthed nurse at the door. Stopping at the now empty desk, he found a yellow post-it note, wrote his number down calmly, and stuck it on the phone the nurse had used to make the call to the doctor in charge.

His footsteps echoed along the corridor back through the door he'd entered through earlier, and past the nurse's station where he'd met the first nurse.

He walked with confidence, assured that the day would go according to his schedule.

Fly in, fly out.

No hovering, no delay, get the job done and go back to the life he'd made for himself.

There was no longer one nurse sitting there, but three.

They all fell silent, all staring, and all giving a disdainful look to the man with the cold interior, but he didn't give a flying fuck. They knew nothing about him and they certainly seemed to know nothing about *her* – the woman lying in the bed, taking up space that a worthy person should have.

Taking the stairs two at a time, he bypassed the full café and broke out into the warm air.

It was only then he unclenched his fists.

It was only then he allowed himself to let go of the breath he was holding.

Taking his secret stash of cigarettes from his back pocket, he lit one up and inhaled the nicotine until it reached his lungs. Retrieving his cell phone from his shirt pocket, he brought it back to life and pressed the third contact name on his favourites list.

"Hey, I'm here," he announced when the phone connected.

"Have you been in to see her?" His aunt held nothing back.

"Yes and no."

"What do ye mean by that? Don't tell me you haven't gone in yet?"

"I have and I am now waiting for the team to get organised. Apparently, they need to speak to me first before I sign anything."

"Well, I guess that would be the right thing to do. They did mention something about that last week. I should have listened more, but so much was going on. Use the time you have to make amends with your mother."

"I have nothing to make amends for, and she surely isn't going to sit up in bed and confess her sins."

"Samuel, that is your mother you're talking about. The only mother ye will ever have. It would do no harm to make the peace. Let bygones be bygones."

"My life is perfect the way it is. Since when was she a mother to me. I had a mother and that was you."

"You've had a strange way of showing you have a mother. Not visiting her would be the greatest sin I could think of. Tell me, are you sitting with her now while ye are waiting?"

At that point, Samuel wanted to lie. He wanted to say yes so he wouldn't have the wrath of his aunt to answer to, but he knew that would be useless. She could sniff out untruth from miles away.

"No, I've popped out to call you and grab a coffee."

"Did you see her at all?"

"No, Aunt Deirdre, and to be honest, I have no intention of doing so."

The phone hummed in his ear. He could hear his

aunt's short breaths and could only imagine how disappointed she was in him.

"I should have never called Thomas away from her side. No one should be on their own."

Samuel could hear movement down the phone and then a door slamming closed. "I'm on my way and you better have finished that coffee by the time I get there. One way or another, you are going in to see your mother." And then the phone went dead.

The coffee in the hospital café tasted diluted. Samuel drank it fast needing the caffeine, but the fruit scone he'd thought he could stomach sat on the plate, untouched.

When he went back for a refill, he asked for an extra shot of coffee, hoping that would make a difference. He should have stayed at the hut by the sea and called the hospital from there. He could cope with the salt filling his nostrils and the serene views much better than waiting for his aunt to march him back to the room again like a child.

Deirdre didn't have wings, but she got there in record time. Samuel thought about having another sneaky smoke before she arrived and chewing some gum to hide the smell from her, but as he got to the entrance, his aunt met him with a red face and puffy cheeks. Deirdre gave him one look that told him everything, and he stepped in line with her through the corridor to the elevators.

"Did you drive or fly here?" he asked, wanting to break the ice.

"Don't be ridiculous, Samuel. I came by car. Thomas drove. He said I was in no fit state to be behind the wheel and by God, he was right. Ye should thank him later for being the recipient of my anger."

Deirdre blew the air from her mouth, getting out the words that must have been stewing during her journey. Samuel hated the thought of upsetting his aunt. In some ways, she was still a mother to him. Never one for sitting on her lap or receiving hugs in his youth, he'd preferred the simple gesture of a ruffle of the hair or a touch of the hand. They meant just the same.

Before the elevator arrived, he knew he had to confront her, to stop this fast and be in control of this shit situation. The thought of upsetting her again, face to face, of seeing the disappointment he knew she'd worn many times because of him, became harder with each passing second.

"Deirdre, I'm not going back up there to sit with her. I'm sorry that my name is down as next of kin. If I could change that, I would, but she doesn't deserve me spending any amount of time with her. The nurse can call me when the team has arrived." Samuel kept his tone low but stern, leaving no room for questions.

Deirdre turned her head to look at him for the first time since she'd arrived in a rush. Her eyes looked tired, the dark shadows underneath even darker than before.

"I should never have sent you that letter. I hoped that

you would come and make peace with Angela, *my sister*, *your mother*, but ye are no different from your father and his selfish ways. Go, Samuel. Go back to the big city and I'll ask the nurse to fax the paperwork to you if that is how strongly you feel."

A tear dropped from the corner of her eye and Deirdre wiped it away with the back of her hand, not breaking her focus on Samuel. Her chest heaved and he could see her hand shaking when she removed it from her face.

"I'll be in the car," he said, then turned his back on her and walked away. Strangely, the only thing that bothered him about her outburst was the remark about his father. Deirdre had never mentioned him before, even when he'd asked many times in the past. Her hands would always fly up, and he'd quickly learnt that the subject was closed.

Time seemed to jump forwards from when he sat in the car, he turned on the local radio and dozed off until he heard his cell phone vibrate in his pocket. He stretched his arms above his head and opened the window a few inches to let some air into the confined space. The person on the other end of the phone sounded impatient when he finally answered. He listened, not wanting to interrupt the caller while he received the information he was waiting for. He gave a brief thank you, checked his rough appearance in the rear-view mirror and got out of the car. Since he'd woken that morning, he looked like he had aged five years. He was sure he could see more grey hairs, and yet inside, he felt like he had gone back twenty. He hoped in the next hour or so, his life would go back to normal and he could pack to return home. But somehow, that seemed too easy.

Nine

Orla watched Samuel approach the desk. Sons like him made her blood boil. Spoilt, thought the world owed him everything, and yet when his mother had needed him weeks ago, he was nowhere to be seen. She would have loved nothing more than to tan his arse and tell him exactly how much that woman had cried when she first arrived there, repeating his name over and over. She'd wailed during the night, asking for someone, anyone, to find her missing son, her first born. Relief had taken over when the medication had been increased and made her drowsy. She'd slept most of the day. The tears that left her eyes were silent and gathered on the pillow beneath her head.

Orla had questioned if there really could be a missing son when none came, but eventually she learned that *he* had yet to be informed of his mother's condition. When Angela had slid into a coma, he had needed to be found.

What person wouldn't want to know about his mother's terminal illness from the moment she arrived in the hospital? Orla couldn't understand. She'd expected his arrival to be emotional, not what she had witnessed.

"Where is the team?" Samuel asked as he approached the desk, not waiting for the nurse to speak first.

"They are in the family room. Take the last door on the left and knock before you enter," Orla replied quickly. Being this close to him made her want to find a ruler to discipline him.

"Thank you," he uttered and left the nurse's station to find the room.

Samuel gave the door with the faded gold sign stating *family room* one solid knock. Turning the handle, he entered without waiting to be summoned. The room, decorated in soft furnishings, tried to give the impression of comfort but failed. Soft chairs with high backs were scattered in pairs, together to share the pain of bad news or the heartbreak of the cold walls and hospital smells.

The small, round table in the centre housed a thick, open file, and there were a few leaflets stacked to one side. A gentleman in a black suit, sitting facing the door, stopped talking and rose from his chair. He extended his hand for Samuel to shake. Samuel walked towards him, his own outstretched hand ready to connect. They nodded, both hiding the inconvenience of the day in smiles that didn't reach their eyes.

The man introduced himself as Doctor Niall Doyle, the leading doctor in his mother's case. Samuel politely thanked him for agreeing to meet on such short notice. Once they were seated, Samuel learnt the names of the team around the table and their roles in Angela's care.

Samuel listened, out of politeness, to what signing the forms would result in.

Yes, he knew his mother was only alive because of the breathing apparatus.

Yes, he knew that it could take minutes or hours before she would actually pass.

He didn't care.

When the team had finished explaining all the legal documents, he only asked one question.

He needed to know if there was any chance at all that she could start breathing by herself.

Niall Doyle talked at length about how it wasn't possible. Any activity in her brain had died. The haemorrhage had made sure of that.

Samuel smiled to himself – a small but significant smile.

In the weeks before Angie's downturn, the team had formed to help with her condition. It had started with a mild stroke. At her young age, the recovery should have been just a few weeks, but the scans revealed something much more sinister hiding behind it all.

The call went out for the family to be gathered. Angela Delaney fell into a coma. Her brain swelled with the pressure and her time had become limited. Switching off her life support sooner would have been a relief, humane, the right thing to do. Waiting until Samuel arrived was torture.

The nurse sitting to his right explained that they'd found an organ donor card in Ms. Delaney's belongings. Tests showed that her organs could give someone else hope, but they needed his permission. The law in Ireland stated that the next-of-kin had the final say.

Samuel sat up straighter in his chair. The thought of anyone having parts of that woman inside them made his blood run cold.

"So you are saying that I could refuse the organ donation?" he questioned, turning his head to look straight at the nurse.

"I am, Mr. Delaney, but we, as a team, hope you give permission. There are many people waiting to enjoy their lives who have been on the list for many years. Some have to attend clinics miles from home for treatment to keep them functioning. It is your mother's wish."

Samuel didn't have to think for another moment. The mention of his mother's wishes sealed the decision for him. He straightened up on the chair to increase his height and authority in the situation.

"*She* will not be having her last wish granted," he replied sternly. "But I will do this for her. Her body can go to medical research at any of the universities in Ireland. The students there can hack away at her flesh, awkwardly cut her with their shaking hands, and if they find a heart, they can slice it and watch the black blood inside seep out. That is what she can have. That can be her dying wish." Samuel waited. He would get this even if he had to fight it through the courts.

The room fell into shocked silence. Hands flew to the mouths of those sitting uncomfortably around the table. Out of the five people who formed *the team*, only one had their gaze fixed on Samuel. The others either shifted in their seats awkwardly or found something in front of them to fiddle with.

Doctor Niall Doyle cleared his throat. "Mr. Delaney, although our universities would be extremely grateful for the generous offer, the donation of a body can only come from the donor themselves. Ms. Delaney has not, to my knowledge, signed the documents for this request."

"Well that is a shame," Samuel replied, rapidly thinking of what to do with her. "In that case, she will need to stay in your morgue until I make arrangements for her body."

Niall Doyle wasn't a man who listened to gossip, but he knew there was no love lost between his patient and her son. Today had certainly confirmed that. He made a mental note to call his own mother when he finished work and accept the invitation for Sunday dinner that he had been putting off for a long time.

After another thirty minutes, all the paperwork was

signed and everyone got up to leave. Samuel shook hands with the staff out of politeness and started to leave the room. Niall Doyle walked with him, stopping just before Angela's door where the others were waiting.

"Mr. Delaney, we are going to start the procedure. Would you like to come in?"

"I think I have done my job here today, Dr. Doyle."

"In that case, I will say my goodbyes to you here and hope you have a safe journey home."

Samuel nodded and started his walk back to the car, satisfied his job was done. As he passed his mother's room, the door was held open by one of the nurses waiting for the doctor to enter. Samuel could hear his aunt's cries but he never turned his head.

Ten

"Are you already packed?" Dee stood in the doorway of Samuel's bedroom. The toddler was resting on her hip, her hair held tight in his fist.

"Well, the deed is done. Time to head home and get back to work."

"But, Samuel, what about the funeral? Ye have to stay for that. I thought you would be here at least until next week. Change your flight, please." Dee winced when Tadgh pulled away his hand and held him closer.

Samuel zipped up his bag and sat down on the bed, before putting the bag on the floor and signalling Dee to sit next to him.

"Dee, there won't be a funeral."

"Holy Jesus, there has to be."

"Not this time, not yet anyway. Not until I know where she deserves to be."

Dee's mouth dropped open and she clasped her hands over the toddler's ears.

"Feck. No. You can't do that. Mam will die when she hears. Samuel, call the hospital and change it. You'll break Mammy's heart."

"She will get over it. Anyway, think of the money I have saved."

"Holy God, have ye no ounce of decency? Aunty Angela is Mammy's sister. She will need a grave to visit over here."

"I don't think a grave is a good idea. Cremation sounds like a worthy send off and empty her ashes far and wide."

"Samuel, that is cruel. I have never heard anyone with no empathy over a loved one before. It disgusts me. You know what, feck off back to that hell of yours, and don't come back unless you find that cold stone heart of yours."

Samuel could hear Tadgh whinge with the speed Dee left the room. She didn't understand. Her tender years had been filled with love and siblings.

His was totally the opposite.

When he'd moved into the Walsh family home, he'd refused to talk about what his house had been like. He hadn't even muttered his mother's name in all the years he'd lived with Dee and her sister.

To him, Angela had died years before.

Samuel didn't wait for his aunt or uncle to return to the house before he left an envelope containing some money for his stay and any inconvenience Angela had caused. He didn't want to see what state he had put his aunt in, or to see the disappointment in Thomas' eyes when he confronted him. Instead, he got into the silver car, threw his holdall into the back seat and started up the engine, taking a last look at the house he thought he would never see again.

In just over twenty-four hours since arriving in Ireland, he had managed to drive a bigger wedge between him and his homeland.

He had over four hours to wait at the airport after returning the hire car, but he much preferred sipping good coffee and having a bite to eat than being back at the Walsh's. Securing a seat in an airport café, he took out his cell phone and scrolled through his messages, deleting the unimportant ones after reading them.

Until he opened the next.

If Dee could have felt his heart, she would have known it was alive. The muscle pumped hard in his chest, the blood racing around and ringing in his ears. A bead of sweat fell from his brow. He read the words over and over, trying to make them change, to form into new ones, but they wouldn't. They still said the same thing, no matter how he looked at the black letters on the pale white screen.

Samuel powered off his cell phone, threw it into his holdall and took out the letter that had caused his change in behaviour and now that text.

Taking the crumpled paper out of the envelope, he

laid it on his thigh and tried to smooth the page with the palm of his hand. His aunt's writing had always been neat. He'd lost count how many times he had read it, trying to decide on the right thing to do. The beginning started like thousands of other letters to family members. *Dearest Samuel.* His aunt didn't fluff around the subject; in the second line, she hit him.

It is your mother. She needs you.

He scoffed at the words Mother and need. He remembered the few times in his life he'd thought he needed his mother but she was nowhere to be seen. Deirdre was the one who had soothed his nightmares and steered him the right way.

Please come back to Ireland before it is too late. The doctors have told me that eventually, she will need to be put on a ventilator, and then it will be down to you to sign her release papers.

Make amends now, Samuel. For your sake and your future. Surely after staying away for so long, you will come back for this.

The doctor has said there is about a two to three-week window of opportunity for you to be here. After that, it will be just your signature they need and your last goodbyes to her shell.

Don't disappoint me and don't leave this to the last moment. What happened in the past should be left there. Your mother had her own problems no one could resolve – a free spirit I think it is called. You have done well, so you have nothing to complain about.

I expect you to do the right thing and contact me with your flight details. Thomas or I could pick you up from the airport and take you straight to Angela.

Now I must end this letter so I can make the post office collection on time. Thirteen years has been too long. Don't delay.

Love,

Aunty Deirdre

xxxxx

Samuel reread the sentences that had been playing on his mind. *What happened in the past should stay there. You have done well, so you have nothing to complain about.* What planet was his aunt on when she wrote that? Did she really believe that his past meant nothing? Hadn't it made him the man he was today? Was she blinded by her blood link to Angie, or did she really believe that he could forget the disgusting feelings that crept into his stomach whenever *her* name was mentioned?

He had left it until the final day of the three weeks before he booked his ticket, hoping to receive a text telling him not to bother. But he didn't have that kind of luck in his life and the flight had to be booked.

Fuck it, he inwardly cursed. He wished he'd never bothered and left her to stew longer in the state she was in. Suffering was exactly what she deserved, but he wouldn't have been able to live with his aunt's haunting words if he had done that. He should have manned up and stayed. Deirdre would be fuming over the turmoil he had left behind. He would call her from the safety of his apartment in a couple of days, explain why he had done what he did and eventually talk his way into her heart again.

Folding the paper back into the envelope, he put it back into his holdall with his cell phone and went to the bar for a whiskey, feeling very much the fucked up man he had hidden for so long.

Eleven

"What do you mean, you texted him?" Chloe stood in the small but functional kitchen while Faye slouched at the breakfast bar.

"I think I've messed up again."

"Why? Don't tell me you sent a message after you left Lewis and me last night in the bar." Chloe balanced her coffee mug on her arm, which was folded across her chest.

"I texted this morning. I couldn't sleep last night. The past three weeks kept going over and over in my mind. I just couldn't stop myself. My fingers typed the words before my brain could think and before I could stop, I pressed send."

"But I thought you two were okay, that when he returned things would go back to normal. Please don't tell me you took Lewis' words to heart. You guys are in a normal relationship. Normal for you both."

Faye gently banged her forehead on the counter top then lifted her head with her hair straggling over her face.

"He makes me so mad sometimes," she wept. "I want to be with him, I want to have a future with him, but not like this. Not with this heavy cloud hanging over our relationship. No love is worth all this hurt."

Resting her tear-stained face in her folded arms, Faye sobbed silently. Rubbing her back, Chloe hushed her friend to soothe her.

"Did he text you back?" she asked, biting her lip and hoping he had for her friend's sake.

Faye shook her head. Chloe moved the dark hair from the side of her friend's face and leaned down towards her ear. "Come on, Faye. Go and have a shower, clean yourself up, change into one of those pretty dresses and come out with me," she said softly, resting her palm on Faye's back.

Turning her head to face Chloe, Faye sniffed then wiped her eyes. "Where are we going?"

"The park. It's a lovely day and I am not wasting my Sunday stuck inside. Bring your bag. We'll head off to the pub for lunch, too."

Sitting upright on the stool, Faye swivelled on the seat looking confused. "What happened to Lewis this weekend?"

Chloe took Faye's small hands in hers, standing in front of her. "Well, after last night, we both thought you needed my company more. And seeing you this morning only confirms my thinking, so get off your arse and get changed."

"Thank you," Faye said, wrapping her arms around Chloe's waist. "Thank you for being here."

"Ah go on. Get ready before the weather changes."

Slipping off the stool, Faye hugged her friend again and moved her unsettled body towards the bathroom.

The sun was high in the sky by the time Faye and Chloe's stomachs were rumbling, and they headed off to The Grapevine after their walk in the park.

Neither of them wanted to sit inside while the weather was so nice. After they ordered their drinks and toasted sandwiches, they sat on one of the wooden benches at the front of the premises.

Picking at the ham hanging out of the side of the toastie, Faye fixed her eyes on a tall, broad, blond man in straight legged jeans and a t-shirt sporting some indie band she hadn't heard of. He was strutting around in front of their seats. Chloe stopped talking mid-sentence and followed Faye's gaze.

"Shit, he looks hot in daylight."

"Close your mouth, Chloe."

"But seriously, I would definitely wrap my legs and more around him."

"Hold up. I need to speak to him." Faye dropped her barely eaten sandwich back on the plate, stepped out of the seat and skipped to catch up with him. Reaching out her hand, she connected with his arm, making him spin around, knocking her off balance.

"Oh God, sorry, love. I thought you were a mugger." Kirk steadied Faye while she replaced the shoe that had fallen off during the collision.

"Totally my fault, Kirk. I didn't want to miss the chance to talk to you, and, well, I should have just shouted your name instead of assaulting you." Hopping on one leg, Faye slipped her shoe back on and used his arm for balance.

When she let go to regain her footing, Kirk waved his hand to respond to the madly waving Chloe still on the bench.

"She with you?"

Faye turned to look in the direction Kirk was pointing, "Yeah, that's Chloe. You know her from The Anchor, but you might not recognise her sober." Faye laughed a little, squinting her eyes against the sun.

"You look well, Faye. Missed you around the bar lately. Everything good by you?"

"Everything is great. Work has been busy. You know how these things get."

"Yeah, but what about the boss? If you don't mind me saying, he has been looking like a right dog's dinner lately. You two haven't had a barney, have you?"

"No, no fight, but you know Samuel – doesn't say much, keeps his thoughts to himself."

"I didn't mean to stick my oar in there, but you know he is like a brother to me and you, well you are so good for him."

"Look, I stopped you, Kirk, because I wanted to know if you had heard from Samuel since Friday?"

"Friday? Yeah, I called him yesterday. Some package arrived and needed his signature."

"And he sounded okay?"

"Sounded fine to me, but I thought you two were together. It's not like him to take the day off without letting me know. I guessed he went somewhere with you."

"If you see him, could you text me?" Faye pleaded, hoping she didn't sound desperate. She didn't want to confront Samuel herself, but she did want to know he was okay, even if she didn't have that right anymore. After the text she'd sent him, she couldn't blame him.

"Of course, I will. Don't be shy, though. Come over during the week. We could chat while Samuel silently stares at you all night."

"Yeah, maybe. Look, I better get back to Chloe. She will start melting from the sun setting if I don't."

Leaning forward, Kirk left a friendly kiss on Faye's flushed cheek and said his goodbyes. Faye watched him. He was carefree and handsome, a man who broke many girls' hearts in the nicest way. He was Samuel's trusted employee and friend, as close as anybody got to him.

She envied Kirk.

She envied his relationship with Samuel.

Anytime the two men had a disagreement, they

argued then drunk away their differences. To Faye, that was better than the quiet lack of communication and the uncertainty.

Samuel had answered his phone to Kirk, but her text went unanswered. His silence spoke volumes to the thousand shattered pieces of her already fragile heart.

Twelve

Samuel walked into The Anchor and threw his holdall on the bar, reaching into the cooler to retrieve a beer. The liquid hardly touched the inside of his mouth before he swallowed. Tipping his head back, he finished the bottle, aimed it at the bin, threw it in and got another.

The door to the cellar squeaked opened, stopping Samuel mid-drink. He waited, the bottle barely touching his lips, as the tall, blond man, carrying mixers, pushed the door open the rest of the way with his foot.

"Well hello, stranger. Thirsty are you?" Kirk smirked at him, resting the box on the floor.

"Yeah, fucking parched." Samuel swigged the drink back, this time holding it in his mouth for a few seconds.

"Have a good weekend, bud?" Kirk began putting the bottles in the cooler, moving the drinks around to make room.

"Just the best, Kirk," Samuel answered sarcastically.

"Any chance it involved the lovely Faye?" Kirk

provoked, prodding Samuel for his reaction.

"Something like that. I'll be in my office if you need me," Samuel responded, filling his arms with as many beers as he could carry.

"Are you drinking all of them and then working tonight, boss? You know the rules," Kirk asked, watching Samuel trying to balance another bottle and failing. "Jesus, Sam, you look like shit." Kirk couldn't hold the words back. They tumbled out once he stood up and looked at the drawn man in front of him.

"Thanks, arsehole. Don't forget to lock the door on your way out. I'll see you tomorrow." Samuel moved away from the bar and disappeared into his office, leaving Kirk watching him leave.

The scream in the dark could only have come from one person. Sweat poured off his body making it stick to the sheet. He held tight to the cotton, his knuckles glowing white in the dark.

Behind his eyelids flashed images he fought hard to make sense of, but he couldn't grasp the facts. The fear and dread were throwing him deeper and deeper into a dark tunnel that made his chest pound. He wanted it to stop. He needed to wake up and get another drink. He needed to drown out these feelings. He needed to wipe Angie Delaney from his memory.

The churning of his stomach woke him and he bolted

for the bathroom before the contents of his gut landed on the floor.

Sliding down the side of the toilet, he wiped his mouth with the back of his hand and rested his head on his bent knees, closing his eyes before blacking out.

The sun beamed through the frosted glass onto Samuel's aching body. Straightening his legs, he winced at their stiffness and rubbed them to ease them back to life. Steadily, he got up, using the basin as leverage, flushed the toilet and faced the mirror above the sink.

"Fuck, you do look like shit," he told himself, sticking out his tongue to inspect it. Shaking his head at his reflection, he splashed his face with water to wake himself up.

He needed a shower. He stunk like a skunk and felt as shitty as he looked. He was glad he had the bedroom attached to his office. It had served its purpose many times over the years, but since he'd got together with Faye, only she had used it.

To him, she was an angel. Every time he wrapped his arms around her, he could feel her heartbeat. Every one of those beats was for him.

Turning on the shower, he waited for the water to heat before stepping under and letting the powerful spray hit his body. Closing his eyes, he thought about the last time he'd taken Faye against the tiles. The memory was etched in his mind forever.

Her innocence entranced him.

Her skin had been soft under his touch and made him burn with the urge to take her a hundred different ways.

She was his.

But he hadn't even told Faye about the darkness that was eating him inside. He couldn't risk losing her. He couldn't risk the future he wanted with her.

But he had.

Receiving that letter from his aunt had made his head clog up. The old knot in his stomach had risen. The devil inside him wanted to do things to Faye he knew she may not be ready for. Not yet anyway, not until he could trust himself.

He'd made an excuse to only see her at the weekends after the letter had arrived. He'd thought the time apart during the week would lessen his urges, but the letter only brought his need closer to the surface. He had to go and deal with the problem, and to him, Angie was a big problem.

His thoughts travelled to Faye. How he would have loved to use his rope on her delicate skin, leaving indents as a reminder of the pleasure it could bring. His hand gripped the base of his hard cock. He swore at himself that now wasn't the time to be erect, but his control was gone. He needed this. He needed Faye. He tightened his hand, strangling the swelling until it throbbed in his palm. If he had his piece of string now, he would have wrapped it around his balls, containing them in a sling and pulling tight to make the blood thicken around the head of his erection. But he didn't. With the image of Faye spread before him in his mind, he fucked his cock with his hand until his cum sprayed from the tip and down into the drain. Quickly, he washed his sin away, feeling guilty for the act he'd performed when his mind was trapped in the past.

Stepping out of the shower, he dressed in his blue jeans and took one of his t-shirts out of the drawer. There was a bang on the glass that separated the bedroom from his office, then the door opened without permission.

"Thought you would like this." Kirk offered Samuel a mug with steam rising from the top.

"Perfect, you must have read my mind," Samuel replied, taking the mug from him.

"Everything okay with you, Sam?"

"Nothing that the open road won't cure."

"Well, you know where I am if you want to burn an ear."

"Kirk, I am not a woman, you sentimental bastard."

Kirk laughed. "Well, that line works with the ladies."

"Fuck off out of my sleeping quarters, you gangly fucker."

"Leaving now, you miserable git. Oh, by the way, that package I called you about is on your desk. Whoever sent it must be confused. It was addressed to Samuel Delaney, not

Walsh."

"I'll sort it out. Thanks."

"Yeah, unless you gave a different name to a girl and now she wants to send you a box of goodies, like her arm or leg."

"Kirk, thanks for the coffee but your imagination should have been left in the bar."

"Right, boss. Leaving now." Kirk backed out of the doorway, his chuckle echoing in the air.

Once the office door shut, Samuel left the bedroom and cautiously approached his desk and box with the Irish postmark.

The box itself wasn't that big. At the most, it reminded him of his old pencil case, oblong and not very thick. The difference was that he knew his blue biro wouldn't be in it.

Pulling out his leather office chair, he sat down and slowly sipped his coffee, watching the package over the rim. The brown wrapping had tape sticking the ends down, not very neatly, and one of the stamps had been stuck on the edge and flattened down the adjoining side. The price indicated that the package weighed little and he recognised the post office stamp from where he'd passed through only a couple of days ago.

Who had posted it? The question went around and around in his head. Angela Delaney was listed as the sender, but he knew that there was no chance she'd made it to the Post Office. Samuel very much doubted she even knew where he lived. If she did, she'd never used the address before, so why now?

Drinking the last mouthful, he put the mug down and picked up the package, satisfied that Angie had nothing to do with it.

He took the oblong in his outstretched fingers and tested the weight. Something slid inside, tipping the box to one side. Rebalancing it, Samuel looked at the handwritten address. The letters that hung low curved giving the impression of a female's writing. That was when it hit him.

Putting the package back on the desk, he strode to retrieve the holdall he barely remembered bringing in. Rummaging through the bag, he took out the letter and his phone.

Back at his desk, he compared the two addresses side by side. Both were written in black ink, both had a curve in the tail of the letter y, and both looked identical.

"Deirdre, you little devil," he said to the package. "Why didn't you just give me this when I arrived?"

He already knew why, though. His aunt hadn't known if he was going to travel over. It had been three weeks after she sent the letter when he did. This must have been her last attempt to get him over to Ireland to visit his mother. Why she had put Angela as the sender, though, was a question he didn't know how to answer.

Sliding his finger under the tape, he unwrapped the package, revealing a cardboard box inside. Taking a knife from one of the drawers, he cut the last piece of sticky tape holding the lid closed. Samuel lowered his head level with the table and very slowly opened the lid, peeking inside.

In the centre sat something flat, enclosed in bubble wrap. Samuel picked it up and left the item on the desk to reveal a folded piece of paper underneath. Using the point of the knife, he carefully wedged it out of its place. Flattening the paper out on the desk, he knew straight away what was in front of him.

Angela Delaney's Last Will & Testament.

Samuel pushed his chair back with force, and it rolled into the glass tiles to his bedroom. If steam could have come out of his ears, it would have.

Back and forth he paced, flexing and balling his fists with each step. The overwhelming urge to punch something heightened even more when he glanced at the will. What did she have that was worth writing down? And why the hell did his aunt think sending it to him was a good idea?

Snatching his keys off a small hook by the window, he slammed the door of his office closed and locked it. He didn't hear Kirk calling his name as he stormed behind the bar and through the door to the cellar.

Taking two steps at a time, he rushed to put on his gear that was stored amongst the stacked bottles. He pressed a button on his key ring and the double doors swung open slowly. Throwing his leg over the low seat of his pride and joy, he turned the key to hear the roar of the engine.

Pulling in the clutch, he kicked the stand up, placed the tip of his boot under the lever he flicked up to hit first gear. Revving the engine, he let out the clutch and pulled out onto the road.

By the time he clunked into sixth gear, his breathing had returned to normal. He wasn't sure where he was going, but he took the back streets until all he saw were green fields beside the road.

He smiled. He had been on the road for hours, and the sun had started to set. He knew there was only one place he needed to be and he didn't give a shit if he was welcome or not.

The spin had cleared his head somewhat. The air flowing against his face felt good. His *Hog* hadn't been out for a while and they both felt better for it.

Pulling up at the curb, he kicked the side stand down and stepped off the bike. Leaving his helmet and gloves resting on the back, he made his way up the path and pressed the intercom of a random number. He gave a poor excuse about a lost key, and the resident mumbled some words of annoyance before buzzing him in.

He had been to this apartment many times, first as the friend that he had been, and then the boyfriend he'd become.

Leaning against the doorframe, he tapped on the

burgundy door and waited with his ear pressed up against it. Nothing. There wasn't even the sound of a door slamming, so Samuel knocked harder.

Still nothing.

Lifting up the letterbox flap, he crouched down and looked through the opening. The place was in darkness except for a glow coming from the sitting room area, but there was no movement. Samuel banged again, this time shouting Faye's name through the opening when he saw a moving shadow.

"I know you are in there, Faye. Open up," he demanded.

The shadow moved closer to the door, paused halfway and then continued, stopping before sliding down level with him.

"No, Samuel, go home." Faye's voice cracked.

"Don't do this. Let's talk things through."

"About what, Sam? I don't know what is going on in that stubborn head of yours, but I have been here to talk for the past three weeks. Where were you then? Not here with me."

"Come on, babe. Don't give up on me. I'm sorry I've screwed up again. Let me in."

"If I let you in, I'll forgive you and we will end up in bed. I know that and so do you."

"What do you want me to do? Tell me," Samuel pleaded through the door.

"Samuel..." Faye lowered her voice through the letterbox. "I want you to go home and think about what you actually want, because right now, I don't think it's me."

Samuel began to respond, but Faye pushed the opening closed with her hand, nearly trapping his fingers in the process. Shaking his hand, he shot up, swore, and kicked the wall with his foot.

"Fuck this shit. Fuck this crazy fucked up world," he spat out at the closed door. He stormed down the stairs and out of the premises, slamming the steel front door closed behind him.

He could hear someone shouting above, but didn't look back to see who he had disturbed. Straddling the black leather seat, Samuel lifted the visor of his helmet, put on his dark glasses and started the engine. The machine vibrated between his thighs, roaring when he turned the throttle back towards him and steered the *Harley* one hundred and eighty degrees round. The sound of the bike could be heard long after he left the street and joined the evening traffic.

He was mad at himself for being back where he'd started at the office.

He was mad at himself for going to see Faye when he knew he wasn't ready.

And he was mad at his mother for making him feel like a screwed up kid in a big, bad world again.

Thirteen

Kirk stood back from the crates of empty bottles, moving away from the door when it opened behind him. Samuel rolled in his bike, switched off the machine and removed his helmet.

"Good ride out?" Kirk asked, testing what mood his boss had returned in.

"Fucking wonderful." Kicking down the stand, Samuel let the bike list to the side.

"It's going to be a quiet night tonight, only the usual gang in using the floor space for their meetings and such."

"Got to keep the business open, Kirk, even if it is the diet bar. Plus, if they have lost weight, they buy more snacks." Taking a cloth from the shelf, Samuel began to buff the chrome on the back of the bike, waiting for the exhaust to cool.

"I'll be cool to work the bar on my own tonight if you need to take time out," Kirk suggested, watching the way Samuel smoothed his cloth over his *Harley*. "You know whatever has got under your skin lately would have been dealt with if you treated the problem like your bike."

"What the fuck are you talking about, Kirk?" Samuel stood from his crouched position, throwing his cloth down on the seat.

"Look, man, I'm not treading on ice around you, but something has got your goat. Your fucking miserable face has been turning away punters."

"Fuck off, will ya? Maybe it's you and all the notches on your bedpost. All the women around here are probably talking about your little penis."

"Awe, fuck, that is cruel, man."

"Well, the truth often is."

"I've got work to finish. You can keep rubbing your ego on your chrome." Kirk didn't wait for a reply. He knew if he stayed, he would probably be out of a job or have a black eye, neither of which he needed.

The bar filled up more than Kirk expected for a Monday night. Not only did the diet group meet up, but a group of workers arrived to celebrate a big deal made that day. The music over the system was a mix of old tunes with new, in keeping with the clientele. Kirk didn't expect anyone to use the dance floor so he kept the music quieter than he would at the end of the week. So, it surprised him when four young women took to the floor and started to swing in time to the music. Turning up the volume a few notches, Kirk wiped the washed glasses and watched the way the woman with long, dark hair swung her hips.

He didn't see Samuel in the corner of the room, pouring another drink from the whiskey bottle he'd taken from the cellar earlier.

The music changed pace and the woman Kirk had been watching approached the bar. Her hair was stuck to her forehead and she brushed it back with her manicured fingers. The buttons of the pale blue shirt she was wearing gaped as her chest heaved to catch her breath.

"Wow, that was exhausting," she puffed out, sitting up on a stool.

"Thirsty work?" Kirk asked, leaning on the bar with his hand stuck in a glass.

"Very. I need to join a gym. I'm so unfit," she panted, her cheeks red and shiny.

"You look mighty fine to me," Samuel interrupted and winked at her.

Kirk turned to his boss. Samuel's eyes looked glazed over and he had a slight stagger in his step. The young woman blushed, the red covering her face completely. Manoeuvring his body between the bar and Samuel, Kirk could smell the liquor on his boss' breath and knew it spelt trouble.

The day he'd walked into The Anchor, fresh off the plane after travelling Asia, his backpack still filled with dirty washing and foreign smells, Kirk stumbled onto

Samuel's path. Some cheeky freshman, wearing a suit he hadn't yet grown into, had been shouting his mouth off after too many daytime drinks and trying it on with the young girls that worked in the bar. Samuel wasn't having any of it.

At the weekend, his bouncer would have dealt with the problem but midweek, the place should have been quiet.

Midday, even quieter.

One thing that annoyed Kirk more than anything was a woman not being treated right.

To him, they were mystical.

The way their bodies moved.

The way they could sweet-talk.

The way they smelled.

There wasn't one part of women he didn't love, and when a man mistreated a woman, he had to step in.

That night, though, he stepped in, not to rescue a woman, but a foolish man.

Samuel had the young man up against the wall by his throat, reading him the riot act. The foolish fresh face turned purple, his legs trying to grip the floor that he couldn't reach.

It took all of Kirk's strength to pull Samuel's hand away from the man and let him go. It took a few glasses of the hard stuff to calm Samuel afterwards.

At that point, Kirk had thought Samuel was in the same league as himself, treating women like Gods. But lately, from the interaction he'd seen between Samuel and Faye, he thought maybe he had been wrong.

The young woman at the bar looked between the two men. Testosterone was radiating from them both. Hesitantly, she asked if she could order a drink, pulling Kirk's attention back to her. He poured the white wine she ordered into a glass, giving her a broad smile, and offered it on the house. She left to join her friends who were huddled in their seats.

Turning back to Samuel after watching the woman walk away, he looked at his friend in disgust.

"Go back to your office, Samuel. You are a fucking mess."

"I would have done, but you scared that gorgeous woman away."

"Don't be fucking stupid. You have Faye, and if she saw the mess you are in she would have something to say."

"Everyone has something to say to me, don't they? I don't think Faye would give a shit right now."

"Is that so? Maybe if you weren't such a dick then she would be with you. Go and sleep this off, Samuel. You're no good to anyone like this."

"Yep, you're right. I'm no good to fucking anyone."

Kirk watched Samuel stagger back out from behind the bar and slowly make his way to the office. He hoped whatever had messed up his head would be sorted before he drank the bar dry. Stress and alcohol combined could only lead to one thing.

A downward spiral.

Fourteen

Since Samuel had left that morning, he had avoided going back into the office to face the demon on his desk, opting for a bottle to keep him company instead.

Turning the key, he opened the door and stumbled into the office. The room looked hazy through his alcohol-fuelled vision, and the package contents were still scattered on his desk, much to his disappointment.

Walking unsteadily and knocking against the furniture to reach his leather seat, he took the weight off his feet and slouched down. Picking up the A5 piece of paper, he began reading through glazed eyes.

The format read like any standard will, and Samuel scanned down to the part where his name alone was mentioned.

Samuel James Delaney, only son of Angela Margaret Delaney.

Samuel repeated the name James over and over in his

head. It was a name he had never been told about before. His birth certificate only stated two names – his forename and *her* surname. Was it his father's name? Why hide the bastard's identity until her death? So many questions ran through his foggy head that it hurt.

The only person who would have the answers, he couldn't call. Not after the way he'd left Ireland and the upheaval he'd walked away from. He doubted his aunt would even talk to him again. No, these questions would have to wait.

On a notepad, he wrote down the name James and underlined it several times until the pen marked the page underneath. Ripping it off the pad, he folded it several times and pushed the paper into his pocket. Picking up the will again, he finished reading it.

The whiskey sitting at the bottom of his stomach kept his blood from boiling. Dropping the page onto the desk again, he slouched back into the seat holding the small, bubble wrapped item he'd retrieved from the package earlier.

Finding the start of the seal, he unwound the tape, unravelling the contents until he was left holding the item between his finger and thumb.

The silver key felt alien in his hand. He held it up to the light and turned it around.

One single key that now belonged to him.

A key that belonged to a holding.

The small, run-down cottage that had once belonged to his Uncle Seamus now belonged to him. It had never occurred to him, after his Uncle's untimely death, that the house would belong to anyone but his Aunt Deirdre.

He hadn't thought Seamus would have even written a will, but he obviously had. Why he'd left it to Angela and not Dee or one of the other girls baffled him.

What good was the house to her? She certainly hadn't lived in it, judging by the state of the place. He could never recall visiting his Uncle with Angela in the years he'd lived with her. That had only happened after he had moved in with Deirdre and Thomas.

Samuel stretched in the chair, rocking his head left and right to ease the pain that had started to settle there. After a while, he rose and took his wallet from his back pocket to pop the key inside, keeping it safe from the urge to flush it down the toilet.

The last few days had started to wear on him. His mouth tasted bitter, and the need to retrieve the string from his holdall and use it made his deflated cock stir.

He stumbled from behind the desk, and in his alcohol infused state, he searched through his holdall for the frayed strands. The twines combined extended to over twelve inches long, and they were strong enough not to snap when tightened. The white colour had faded to grey over the years, holding memories in each of its twists. Holding it tight in his fist, Samuel staggered to his bedroom and sat on the edge of his bed. His heart raced, the anticipation of the thrill he would receive deepening his breath and making his palms feel damp. The urge to use the threads increased with every discovery he made about Angela.

Unbuttoning his black jeans, he skimmed them down his strong, bike hugging thighs and kicked them off his feet. He willed his cock to stiffen, promising to give it the relief the string would bring.

Instead, his whiskey fuelled body collapsed onto the unmade bed and he fell into a drunken coma with the string tightly grasped in his hand.

Fifteen

The morning had already passed by the time Samuel opened his eyes, and the taste of death was settling in his mouth. He tried lifting his head only to let it fall back on the pillow. The machine that was pounding in his brain needed to stop. The pain was barely manageable if he kept still.

Samuel could hear a knocking on the office door, but he couldn't answer. He listened until the knocking became louder, silently begging it to stop. A few moments later, Kirk forced the door open and called out Samuel's name.

"In here, Kirk." Samuel quickly covered his naked half with the sheet underneath him, the string forgotten. He barely opened his eyes to see Kirk walk into the room and stand looking disapprovingly at him splayed out on the bed.

"Holy Christ, man. How much did you drink?"

"Too fucking much. Shit, Kirk, my head hurts."

"Oh man, I shouldn't laugh, but right now I would like nothing more than to take a picture of you to show what a lightweight you are."

"Don't you fucking dare. I can drink anyone under the table. I must have picked up a virus or something."

Kirk laughed. "Now you are making excuses."

"What do you want, Kirk?" Samuel asked, wanting the lanky man to leave so he could die in peace.

"Didn't see your ugly mug this morning and thought I had better check you were breathing."

"What time is it?"

"Well past the morning... It's nearly four o'clock, mate."

"Shit! I need to get up and put in an order before the weekend." Samuel tried to move from the bed, but his pounding head wouldn't let him.

"Stay there, boss. I'll bring you a couple of magic pills."

"Magic pills? I hope they are legal."

"Yep, legal alright. Mr. Aspirin, coming right up."

Kirk left the room and Samuel closed his eyes again to stop the bed from spinning. The last time he could recall feeling this bad was when he was a teenager.

He had sneaked a bottle of Thomas' good whiskey from his aunt's cupboard, taken it out in the field behind a haystack and drunk half the bottle before the sun started to set. Deirdre had wailed, begged to know why, what had caused him to drink himself to harm, but he didn't have a clue.

He'd found the bottle and drank it.

His Uncle Thomas had found him after searching all evening. Not once did Thomas raise his voice. He shook his head, and disappointment seeped from his pores.

A cold flannel had been placed over his forehead when he'd stopped puking up the contents of his stomach. His aunt had sat beside him reciting Hail Marys for his sins.

Right now, he really needed that cold flannel and his aunt's prayers to get the poison out of him.

Kirk had left the tablets beside the bed, along with a glass of water and an empty bucket. Before Kirk had shut the office door, Samuel had started to fill the bucket. He swore that whichever company he'd bought that whiskey from would hear about how shit the drink was.

Vowing to change his tipple, he knew he should have kept to the Irish brand that sat on the top shelf in most Irish pubs. But his wasn't an Irish pub and he was determined to keep it that way. From the very beginning he'd refused to go down the route of Irish themed nights, and only on the 17th March would he allow a drink to be raised in honour of St. Patrick. He tried to keep his Irish roots tucked deep under the surface.

However, the deeper he tried to hide something, the thicker its root became, needing to burst through, exposing the real person behind the façade. Nothing stayed hidden for long and Samuel had started to realise that.

Sixteen

A week had passed since Samuel had arrived back from Ireland and five days since he'd punished his knuckles on Faye's door only to be rejected.

Work had been steady over the week and he hadn't returned to finish off the whiskey after the night he'd passed out, but his nightmares had.

He needed Faye more than he'd ever thought he would. Pushing her away had given him no answers. He'd kept his past in a dark corner for so long that he had no idea how to handle it now that his ghosts had caught up with him. He'd carried the hatred he had for his mother with him for so long that when the letter had arrived, brick by brick he'd shut himself off from Faye.

The trip had accomplished nothing.

In his fucked up mind, he'd envisioned the weekend going according to his plans.

Fly out.

Sign papers.

Fly back home.

Nothing in his schedule stated he would lose his girlfriend in the process.

He missed Faye.

He missed her signature flowery perfume, her smart mouth, her ruby lips.

He missed sinking deep inside her, and the sound of her sweet moans for his ears only.

Most of all, he craved the feeling of wrapping his arms around her, stroking her smooth, delicate skin, and telling her he would never walk away again.

But that had disappeared, all because of the stubborn son of a bitch he had become. Or, he thought, maybe he was always that distant. Maybe he'd hidden his true self when he met Faye, and the letter, dripping in his past, had re-surfaced the real him.

A dreaded realisation came over him: if he looked in a mirror, would he see Samuel or his heartless mother? The latter would explain the past month – the actions and decisions he'd made – and that unsettled him.

Was this nature over nurture?

If no one had come beating the door down when he was seven, would he still have become the man he was? The fucked-up, good-for-nothing drifter. Even with a new surname, his soul had waited for the day to remind him where he came from, who had pushed him into the world and whose DNA he shared.

In the early hours, moments after the nightmares, he knew that Faye should stay far away from a messed up man like him.

Seventeen

The weekend buzzed. The punters were many and the booze flowed until the taps ran dry. The summer tried hanging on through the short days, but the autumn fought it. Samuel's life became a circle of work, bike and limited sleep. If he didn't sleep, he couldn't dream and the nightmares lost their chance to claw into him.

He smiled at the customers, grunted at his staff, while his mind clouded with the thoughts of the one he'd lost. He functioned day to day on autopilot with a fiery dark cloud hanging over his head.

"I swear to God, if you look at that door again I'll bang your head off the bar, Sam," Kirk shouted above the Sunday night local band. "Will you just call her and straighten out your shit?"

"What the fuck you on about?" Samuel barked, cocking his head back while pulling a fresh pint.

"Shit, man, Faye! I think I preferred you passed out on the bed than all distant like this."

"Fuck, Kirk, I didn't know you'd turned into a girl. Do you have your period, too?"

Kirk called over one of the younger bar staff, Freda, to take over the payment from Samuel's customer. Pulling him by the elbow, he steered Samuel to the cellar steps. Taking his cell phone from his pocket, Kirk scrolled for Faye's number and then handed the phone to Samuel. Samuel hesitated before gripping his head in his hands.

"Shit, man, I can't. I have nothing to say."

"Call her, Sam. One of you has to make the first move."

Samuel turned away and walked to the top of the cellar steps. He could take them two at a time and be on his bike within seconds – screw the gear, it would take too long. He envisioned grabbing his helmet and riding the beast until... He didn't know until when. He just wanted to get out. He wasn't ready to call her. He didn't trust who he had become.

"Take it, talk, and don't come back into work until you do. Your ugly mug is a distraction."

Samuel slipped his hands to the back of his neck and turned to face his only friend. His head started to hurt. He'd hoped to be numb by now with the mention of her name, but it cut him straight through the heart.

"Calling her won't make an ounce of difference. She won't answer anyway."

"She will. It's my phone."

The knife twisted further into his chained heart. She

133

would see Kirk's name on the screen and answer. He knew that and it hurt.

Samuel took the cell phone from him. Kirk pressed the green phone symbol and smirked, leaving the room to go back to the bar while the phone connected the call.

Holding the phone to his ear, Samuel wiped his free hand down his dark jeans then swapped hands and did the same with the other. He hoped she wouldn't answer, silently begged her not to, but by the third tone, her voice filled his ear.

"Hello, Kirk, what's up?"

Samuel wet his dry mouth with his tongue and let out a nervous cough. "It's Sam, Faye."

"Oh, is Kirk okay?"

"He is fine. He...I had to use his phone. I thought you wouldn't answer if I rang from mine."

"It is kinda late, Sam."

"Oh, I didn't check the time. You must be busy. I'll hang up," Samuel stuttered, wanting to kick the wall for his stupidity.

"No, no, don't. I'm home reading."

Silence hung between them. Samuel leaned his head against the cold, stone wall.

"Samuel, you still there?"

"I...I don't know what to say."

"Maybe saying nothing is best."

"Maybe...Is that what you want?"

"Samuel, that text I sent was for real. I don't know what to say to you anymore. You are so...cold, so shut off."

"I know I fucked up. I'm fucked up. I don't know who I've become or if this is the real me."

"Look, it's too late to talk about this. I'll call you tomorrow, okay?"

"Yeah, sorry. I shouldn't have called. Night, Faye."

"Night, Samuel."

Samuel disconnected the call, skimmed down the stairs and put on his leather jacket, boots and helmet, opening the cellar doors wide.

The *Honda* engine hummed rather than roared like his *Hog* and at that time of the night, it was less noticeable. The whistle of the engine sounded as he warmed her up and he grinned, knocking the gear out of neutral, and rode her out onto the road.

The thirty-minute ride gave him a chance to think of all the excuses he could make before he arrived outside the apartment. The memory of the last time he'd been there left a bitter taste in his mouth but after the phone call, he selfishly had to see her.

Letting the bike tick over before he switched it off, he looked up at Faye's bedroom window. The curtains were closed, and the reading lamp was aglow. Taking the key from the ignition, he stepped off the bike with ease and left the helmet in the back box. The boots weighed his feet down as he slowly made his way up the steps to the steel door. His finger hovered over the apartment numbers, undecided which one to press. It was later than the last time he disturbed a resident and he didn't want an angry person shouting down the intercom, so he pressed number twenty-six and stepped back. Shuffling his feet, he kept his head bowed, wishing he had brought a spare pair of trainers to change into.

"Hello?"

"Hi, Faye, it's me. Can you let me in?"

"Samuel?"

"Yeah, babe, it's me."

"It's late."

"I know, but I needed to see you."

"I was in bed."

"Let me in, babe. I swear I won't stay long."

"Can this not wait until tomorrow?"

"Not this time. Please, Faye, let me in."

Samuel rubbed his forehead with his hand, taking in a breath through his teeth. Begging was not on his agenda. He didn't like it and he wasn't going to do it.

The silence answered when Faye didn't, so, taking his key out of his pocket, he moved away from the intercom and retreated to his faithful *Honda*. His boot had landed down on the step when the distinctive sound of the door unlocking rang in his ears. Samuel hopped back, hurrying back to the door to stop it from closing again.

Faye was standing at the open door to her apartment,

her arms folded across her chest, her feet bare with painted red nails. He tried to gulp down the lump that sat in his throat. She looked like an angel with her hair tussled from her pillow before he'd disturbed her. To Samuel, she glowed, and she made him glow. It took all his willpower not to scoop her up in his arms and kiss her ruby lips. Instead, he inhaled the scent of her hair fresh from a shower as he passed beside her to go inside.

Making his way to her kitchen, he turned on the kettle and retrieved two mugs from the cupboard, filling them both with a spoonful of instant coffee.

"Don't fill my mug. I've already brushed my teeth for bed."

Taking the extra mug back, Samuel waited until the kettle had boiled and filled his before seating himself opposite Faye at the breakfast counter.

"We're not going to sit here in silence while the clock is ticking. I have work in the morning. What couldn't wait, Sam?"

He leaned forward and took his wallet out of his back pocket. Opening it, he retrieved the item he'd put in there earlier and placed it on the counter between them.

"A key? You came here to show me a key?" Faye asked, a little bewildered.

"It's not just any key, Faye. It was left to me."

"By who?"

"A woman by the name of Angela Delaney. Or as I call

her, Angie."

"You don't have to talk about the woman that has got your head in a spin. I don't want to pry, but if you need to talk, I'll be a friend. That is all I can be, though, nothing more."

"I need to explain. Let me."

Faye picked up the key. It looked like any other silver key. She held it up and turned it around. Nothing about it was unusual so she placed it back on the counter and pushed it towards him.

"So you want to talk about a key?" she asked.

"Yes."

"And you couldn't talk to me about this any other time? What has it been, four weeks now?"

"It has been complicated."

"Really? So, let me get this straight. You receive a letter with an Irish stamp, and our relationship starts to become a little strained, to say the least. One minute, you're whispering sweet nothings in my ear and telling me I am your future, blah, blah, blah, and the next, I'm the weekend girl."

Samuel opened his mouth to respond, but Faye put her hand up to silence him having bottled up her anger for too long.

"Wait one minute, mister. You are in my home now so you can hold on to any excuses you have until I am finished."

Samuel took another mouthful of coffee and let her dispel the hatred she had for him.

"I know I am not a therapist or anything, but the nightmares you have been having – and don't try to deny them – only seem to have reared their ugly heads since that godforsaken letter arrived. So, I am guessing whatever was written in there has hit a nerve. I don't know what it could be because, to me, before, you were a man who had no worries or stress. Looking at you now, though, seeing you sitting there all quiet tells me something else. You're fucked up, Samuel, and by the looks of it, it is something big."

Samuel said nothing. He simply picked up the key and placed it back into his wallet. He, of all people, knew she was right, but the right words to explain didn't materialise. Reaching out, he placed his warm hand on top of Faye's.

"Talk, for fuck's sake. Don't just sit there with your moody eyes and your pouting lips."

"I don't have pouting lips."

"No? I'd better get a mirror for you to see."

"I miss you, Faye."

"Oh fuck, we are not doing this, Samuel. Seriously, if this is a ploy to work your way back into my good books, then you had better leave now. I let you in as a friend. Don't take that as a ticket to ride."

Samuel watched as she tucked her hands under her arms. It made him proud to see how strong she was. He knew it wouldn't take much for her to land back into his arms, the way things were.

"I swear it's not. I wouldn't betray your trust like that. You know me well enough. This is exactly why it took me five years to be with you in the first place. I didn't want to ruin our friendship. You were my best friend. You still *are* my best friend. And I need you as my best friend now. I swear, no monkey business."

Faye's shoulders slouched and Samuel could see the tension leaving her body.

"That key," he said, almost in a whisper. "That key was left to me in a will by somebody I have despised for many years. Right now, I don't know whether to throw it in a river, flush it down a toilet or hold on to it."

"Why throw it away? Maybe the person left it to you because they are asking for forgiveness for whatever they have done."

"Forgiveness? I would need more than a key for that."

"So explain again, who is the key from?" Faye's head tilted to the side as she asked the question, willing him to answer and not walk out. She extended her hand out to him for support.

Taking the comfort, he squeezed her hand gently and rubbed his free palm over the back of his neck.

"Angela Delaney is my mother. She didn't treat me in a way a mother should have done."

"Oh God, I am sorry, Samuel. Why have you never told me this?"

"What was there to tell? I was taken away and cared for by my aunt until I was old enough to get out of there and move here. By the time we met, she was a long distance disaster."

"All those years I knew you must have been from Ireland, but you never spoke about it. Why?"

"Didn't come up in conversation, I guess. I tried my best to mimic other accents and tone mine down. Don't get me wrong, I am proud to be Irish. I just didn't want to be asked questions about my past. It's in my Irish nature to not talk about certain things so I didn't. Easier to say nothing."

"Fuck, Samuel, what other secrets are you hiding from me? How old were you when you were taken from your mother?"

"I don't want her to be called my mother. She's not worthy of the title. She's just Angie. She was no mother to me." Samuel flexed his arms above his head. He could feel the tension weighing down his shoulders, but he wasn't going to confess to Faye what he'd done on his quick visit.

"I think I was about seven when I went to live with my aunt. It was all a bit hazy when it happened."

"Do you want to talk about your....I mean Angie?"

"Nope. She doesn't deserve an ounce of my breath."

"So what do you want to talk about? Are you expecting me to tell you what to do with that key?"

"Shit, I don't know. I never asked for this crap to land

on my doorstep. We were fine, weren't we, you and I? I want to go back and burn the letter before I opened it, but that's impossible."

"So maybe we should start at the beginning with what the letter said. Do you want to do that? Tiny steps, nothing heavy."

"Unless you have a magic wand."

"Look, it's too late tonight and to tell you the truth, my mind is exhausted from what you have already told me. Can we do this tomorrow after I finish work?"

"Yeah, and Faye? You know I miss you?"

"You have said that, but you must know why *us* can not happen."

"But it could?"

"Don't push me, Samuel. Tiny steps, remember?"

Samuel couldn't help himself. He leaned forward and brushed his lips across hers, standing up from his seat to reach her.

"I'm leaving," he announced, not wanting to see the pity in her eyes, and left the half-empty mug on the counter behind him. He wished for nothing more than to take her in his arms and carry her to bed. Her lips, forever imprinted on his, made him want more.

Eighteen

"Why are you looking so smug?" Kirk asked when Samuel joined him behind the bar on his return.

"No reason, my man, no reason."

"Nothing to do with that phone call I made you make?"

"Maybe."

"Well fuck, you two are mad for each other. Someone had to knock your heads together."

"Nothing is back on between us, Kirk. We're just friends. That is all."

"Ah, shit. Your dick will be aiming its way back to her. You wait and see."

"Crude talk, my friend. You should wash your mouth out with soap."

"Yeah, we will see."

Samuel walked the short distance back to his apartment a few streets away after the band had left and he'd locked up the premises. He hadn't been back there since he'd left for Ireland, so he opened the window to circulate a bit of fresh air. The place felt dead, unused and silent.

Turning on the TV, he scanned to find a music channel from his era. Slouching on the couch, he kicked off his trainers and put his feet up on the glass coffee table that was overflowing with newspapers and bike magazines. Pushing them around with his foot, he found the one he knew he had left under the pile.

Pulling it out, he flicked through the pages and stopped at the centre fold. He needed to unleash the tension that had been building all evening after seeing Faye. He had found his piece of string on the floor of the office sleeping quarters and held it in his hand now. Unzipping his jeans, Samuel skimmed them down his thighs, kicking them off as they landed on the floor. His cock was hard and ready under his boxers.

Lifting his white t-shirt over his head, he discarded it, then hooking his thumbs into the band of his black boxers, he pulled them wide to let his cock spring free, letting them fall wherever he threw them. He lay back on the couch, positioning a pillow under his head, and began the process of tying the threads around his stiff shaft.

Each loop he made around it, he swelled. He knew this would end fast. The urge to use the string grew stronger the deeper he thought of Faye and what her lips could do to him. His past hovered under the surface, increasing the tension inside him with each twist. Wrapping the last piece around his testicles, he tied a knot to keep the pressure at its peak. Resting back on the cushion, he rubbed his cock, stroking the head in a circular movement then down to the swollen base. With each downward movement, the string tightened. He felt it starting to cut into his taunt skin, but still, he kept going. The blood rushed around his body so fast that he became lightheaded from the pleasure the pain was giving him.

Just when he couldn't hold on anymore, he pulled the small length of string left at the end and unravelled the tension. Pumping his cock with his hand, he came with a deep throaty groan. Sweat beaded on his forehead, and he wiped it away with the back of his hand, unable to move until he regained his breath.

Samuel wrapped the string into a small ball and put it down the side of the couch. Content, he staggered to his bedroom, lay on the bed and was asleep before his eyes closed. His body was satisfied and relaxed for the first time in weeks.

The clock was illuminated in the dark room, Samuel groaned, kicking off the sheet that had wrapped around his legs as he slept. Five o'clock was no time to be awake after only a couple of hours of sleep, but the scene playing in his mind didn't belong there and the soaked sheets beneath him made his anger rise. He'd hoped that talking to Faye after walking away from his home country had done enough to rid him of the flashes of memory that were on repeat, but they'd only grown stronger.

Samuel wiped his face with his hands, rubbed the back of his neck before lowering his head. His bare feet rested on the cool tile floor as he sat on the edge of the mattress and waited to catch his breath before standing. Lately, the time it took to recover after a nightmare had increased, and tonight was no different. He inhaled deeply through his nose and exhaled through his mouth, controlling each intake of air.

He needed a drink. His mouth felt like a desert. He wanted something to make him feel the way he had before the letter, before the trip and before the memories resurfaced. Something strong that would hit the spot in a few mouthfuls.

Racking his brain, Samuel tried to think whether he had any whiskey in the apartment. He had plenty at the bar, but home was another story. He knew there was a bottle of wine in the fridge from the last night Faye had spent there – the night she'd witnessed his nightmare, but he would avoid it, not wanting to be sick from stale alcohol again.

Samuel forced his body off the bed and stomped through the apartment to the fridge, he took out several cans of beer and returned to his room. Passing the door to his lounge, he paused for a moment and guzzled half the first can before coming up for air. He'd left his holdall in there when he'd arrived home earlier. Sitting down on the single chair he pulled the bag between his legs, retrieved the piece of paper from the pocket and unfolded it. Finishing the first beer, he opened another, blinking his eyes a few times to focus on the fancy writing.

Angela's name didn't deserve the tidy writing it was written in. Halfway down the page, he stared at his name. He had been left the cottage, all its contents and the surrounding field. Samuel rubbed his forehead to relieve the headache that was building. The cottage – Uncle Seamus's cottage – the one thing Angela had to leave, had been left to him.

Why was the cottage in Angie's name? He'd always assumed it belonged to his Aunt Deirdre and her family. The whole thing made no sense and left him with a bad taste in his mouth that wasn't from the beer. The last thing he needed was to deal with unanswered questions and a will that he had to go back to Ireland to sort out.

Fuck Angie, he inwardly fumed. Why couldn't she just die and be erased from his memory instead of leaving her death and a fucking house to deal with?

Pushing the legal papers away, he closed his eyes, resting his unshaven chin in his hands. His world had become more fucked up, and once again the problems lay with the woman he had been running from.

Nineteen

"Kirk, I am gonna need to leave you in charge for a few days."

"You disappearing again?" Kirk asked, rearranging the bottles in the fridge behind the bar.

"Have to, man," Samuel answered, keeping his head down while writing out the rosters.

"Same place you disappeared to last time?"

"Yep."

"Don't want to expand on that?"

"Nope. Nothing exciting – just a few strings to tie off." Samuel smirked at his own joke regarding the string, pleased Kirk couldn't see his expression from where he worked.

"Did you find that package on your desk, the one that was addressed to a Mr. Delaney?" Kirk asked, wanting to change the subject.

"I did. Thanks for signing for it."

"So was it yours?" Kirk stopped what he was doing and

leaned against the bar.

"What was in it was mine. I guess they put the wrong name but the right address."

"That is a bit strange, don't you think?"

Putting his pen down, Samuel let out a deep sigh while he thought of a suitable answer to shut Kirk up.

"The person who sent it must have been sending in bulk and got trigger happy with the copy and paste while printing out the labels."

"Did you ring them to complain?"

"Sure did," Samuel lied. He wasn't going to explain to Kirk about his name change. "It won't happen again."

"When are you heading off?"

"Why? You miss me already?"

Kirk snorted. "You fucker, a few days without your ugly face sounds like a holiday to me."

"Yeah well don't get too used to it. This will be the last time I'll be leaving."

"Out of interest, when was the last time you had a holiday from this place?"

"I haven't, Kirk. This is my life. You should know that."

"Yeah, but I thought I would ask. You could have had time off before I arrived."

"Nah, not me. Had to keep my beady eye on the place. I should be keeping it on you, too, but I have been slacking."

"Too many women come in here to see me. To tell you

the truth, you not being here has brought in more punters."

"Fuck off."

"Seriously, check the takings."

"Are there any women left in this town that you haven't slept with?"

"Now you mention it, there is a brunette who comes in every other Friday, but she won't bite my hook."

"Losing your touch are you?"

"I swear my charms are still working, but not on her."

Swivelling in his chair, Samuel faced Kirk, amused.

"Who is this woman who ignores your advances? I want to buy her a drink and put her name on a trophy behind the bar."

"You wanker. Though, if you think it would make her take notice of me then I am in."

Samuel rubbed his fingers over his coarse chin, thinking.

"Friday night, did you say?"

"Yeah, she was here last week."

"Long wavy hair, heels taller than herself and deep red lipstick?"

"God, for someone not interested in other women, you have described her to a tee. Do you know her?"

"Actually, Romeo, I do. I'd give up if I were you. She is out of bounds."

"No woman is out of bounds, Sam. She wasn't wearing a ring."

"Well, I'll leave you to find out who she is then."

"Oh come on, just spill it."

"I have work to do before I leave, and so do you." Picking up the paperwork and the half drunk mug of coffee, Samuel retreated to his office, leaving Kirk with a puzzled look on his face.

Samuel picked up the phone and paused. For a moment he wanted to back out, but he needed to sweep away the mess that was trailing behind him. Clearing his throat, he connected the call.

"Samuel?" Faye's voice was gentle in his ear.

"Faye, I have a question to ask you," Samuel blurted out fast.

"Okay, ask away."

"Can you pack a bag and take a few days off work for me?"

"For what?" Faye asked, a little taken aback.

"I want you to come to Ireland with me," he replied, lowering his voice to a whisper.

"Did I hear you right?"

"As a friend. I want you with me, Faye."

"I don't know. This is really short notice."

"I know, but I wouldn't ask if this wasn't important."

"When are you going?"

"Tomorrow, on the first flight out."

He could hear the rustling of papers while he waited anxiously for Faye's answer.

"Faye?"

"I'm still here."

"You're the only one I wanted to ask."

"And what about the last time when you disappeared without an explanation? How do I know you won't do that when you get there?"

Changing the phone to his other ear so he could wipe the sweat from his brow, he pulled a deep breath into his chest.

"That won't happen again. I promise you that. My mind was a little fucked up then."

"And now?"

"This trip will clear it."

"So why do you need me to go with you? You managed fine without me last time."

"You're wrong there, Faye. I didn't manage at all. To tell you the truth, I don't know exactly what I will be facing when I return, but I want you with me. I need you with me."

"Samuel, you're confusing me. Look, I am still at work and can't talk about this right now."

"Then come with me. It's the key, Faye. I need to find out about the key and why Angie had it."

"The key you showed me?"

"Yes."

"Okay, I'll come with you. But as a friend, nothing more."

"I'll pick you up on the way to the airport."

152

"Not on your motorbike."

"Not on my bike." Samuel's mouth lifted into a grin as he disconnected the call, but it didn't stay there long when he pressed to call Dee.

Before she had even answered, he knew he was going to get a mouthful and Dee didn't disappoint. At one point, he left the phone on his desk and let her rant about the mess he'd left behind. He didn't even try to make excuses. He knew that would have been a waste of breath.

Eventually, when Dee paused, Samuel grabbed the phone back up to inform her that he would be arriving tomorrow and would be bringing Faye. Dee changed her tone when she heard Faye would be travelling with him and offered to put her up in the house, but refused a bed for Samuel. The wrath of his Aunt Deirdre would have him plastered to the walls if he were to enter the house where he was no longer welcome.

Samuel searched the Internet for accommodation in the area while he was still talking to Dee. The only place with two rooms available was The Huddle. His heart dipped as he scanned the pictures on the website.

He knew those rooms all too well.

He thought about only booking one room and letting Faye stay with Dee, but he'd promised to keep her close. He hoped explaining to Dee that if he weren't able to stay with Faye at the farm, then they both would be staying in The Huddle would be enough for her to change his aunt's mind, but it didn't. Instead, Dee agreed that it would be best if they both stayed there. Samuel looked at the screen again. He had no choice. He would have to book it before it sold out like the other places.

He just hoped the ghosts of his past at The Huddle were long gone.

Twenty

The one-hour flight touched down on the tarmac with a bump. Samuel had avoided all conversation about why he was heading back to Ireland for the second time in a month during the journey. He was grateful that Faye hated flying and spent most of the time with her eyes tightly closed and her knuckles turning white, gripping onto the arm of the chair. By the time he had the rental onto the byroads, she'd gained the power of speech again.

"Wow, Samuel, look at the views," She said, opening the window and staring at the landscape.

"Yeah, I know, very green."

"And you left this for the city?"

"Gotta live and see the big world out there."

"Yeah, but I didn't even know you were from somewhere so... What is the word?"

"Quaint?"

"Hmm, yeah, maybe it is quaint. I mean, look at you all rough and ready."

"What the fuck is wrong with me?"

"When was the last time you shaved, Sam?"

"I like it. Don't you?" he asked, taking one hand off the wheel to rub the bristles he had trimmed only a few days ago.

"Honestly?"

"Yeah, go on."

"You look tired. I don't think the unshaven look helps with that."

"Maybe, or maybe you like it but don't want to admit it."

Faye stared back out at the passing fields, leaning her head back against the headrest. They both retreated into their own worlds until they reached the sign that announced they were arriving in ShanInis.

Samuel slowed the car down. He could feel his heart racing in his chest. Gripping the steering wheel tighter, he rolled through the narrow streets overflowing with people.

"Gosh, this is a busy town," Faye remarked when Samuel had to stop to allow pedestrians to get off the road.

"There must be an event on or something," he replied, braking once again to avoid another pedestrian who had stepped off the thin pavement.

"Ooh, look over there, Sam. It looks like there is a festival happening over the weekend."

Samuel directed his attention to where Faye was pointing and his heart sank. There, emblazoned on a banner across the whole street, were the words 'Food Festival'.

Instantly, he wanted to turn the car around, speed out of the small town and away from the weekend long event, but he couldn't. Now he understood why most of the accommodation was booked out.

When he'd lived there, the place had been dead after the summer months. Not much had ever happened unless a film crew found a spot to film the views, but now, for October, the place seemed to be flourishing. The further they drove through the streets, the more excited Faye became, pointing out different advertisements along the way.

"Is this why you brought me here, Samuel, for the festival?"

"If I say yes, will you stop with the running commentary?"

"Did you know it was on? I have never been to a food festival before. The place is buzzing."

"It sure is. Put your phone away, Faye. I'm sure you will be able to take pictures later," Samuel scolded, not wanting anyone to notice him in the car.

"We are coming back to this town then?" Faye asked, putting her phone back into her bag.

"No choice. We're staying just on the outskirts. You can walk back in later while I'll sort some things out if you want."

"Ah, come on, Sam. I know you love food. Surely you want to have a taste."

"There is only one thing I want to taste and unfortunately, it is off the menu."

Samuel could see Faye's cheeks turning crimson out of the corner of his eye, and it made him smile. He liked that he still had some effect on her even though she was doing her best to fight it. Resting her head on the half-open window, Faye stared outside, clearly intrigued by the small but vibrant town.

They checked in at The Huddle and made their way up the stairs to their rooms. Handing Faye her key after he opened her door, Samuel informed her that he needed to take a shower to freshen up and would meet her back at her room in thirty minutes. Faye said she would do the same, but if he wanted to meet her anywhere, it would be in the bar. She was hungry after the journey having skipped breakfast to avoid being sick on the flight. Samuel was about to argue with her when she shut the door in his face, much to his annoyance.

In the bar, Samuel felt like he had been transported back to his teenage years. The walls and the fabric on the seats were different, but the layout hadn't changed. The little snug tucked away in the corner had changed, the cushions now a deep red rather than the bottle green he remembered.

An image flashed through his mind of Molly O'Brien

in her short school skirt, sipping a drink through a straw while her foot rubbed along his leg. His hormones had been on fire. She knew how to tease him, and he loved her for it. Molly only had to flutter her eyelashes at him and he would have done anything for her.

"You want a drink and something to eat?" Faye called to him from the bar, snapping him from the trance he'd fallen into.

"Wha... Yeah, I'll just have a beer. I'll wait outside."

Wanting to get out of the place quickly, he left some money on the counter before the barman arrived.

"Okay," Faye answered and waited to order.

Samuel sat on one of the benches furthest from the road. It didn't take long for Faye to join him, sitting on the opposite side of the table.

"So, what is on the agenda for today?" Faye questioned.

"Lunch, then you can go for a walk around the town while I'll head west."

"And what is west?"

"Home."

Faye placed her drink on the table and looked at him from beneath her fallen fringe. Licking her lips, she skirted the rim of the bottle with her thumb, allowing her shoulders to slouch.

"Home?"

"Yes, Faye, home – where I spent my youth before

159

leaving."

"Do you not want to introduce me to the rest of your family?"

"I will, but not today. I have some grovelling to do."

"In the bad books? Why doesn't that surprise me?"

"What can I say? I drag trouble around with me."

"I don't think you are trouble. You're just always in the wrong place at the wrong time. Have you ever thought before you act?"

"Why should I? This is who I am. If people don't like it, then that is their problem, not mine."

"Do you know how frustrating you can be?"

"Look, Faye, have a walk around the town. Who knows? You might find some decent shops. I'll take a drive and we can meet back here this evening. Sound good to you?" Samuel suggested, diverting away from her question.

"Yeah, sounds like a ball."

"If I were you, I'd find out where your toasted sandwich has got to. Seems like they have forgotten you." Standing up, Samuel took the rental keys from his pocket and leaned forward to kiss the top of her head.

Faye moved out of his way, leaving him to kiss the air instead, and pushed past Samuel to go back to the counter in search of her food.

His promise had fallen by the wayside.

Twenty One

"Was that Samuel Delaney you were just with?"

Faye was sat at the bar, biting into her warm sandwich, looking through the local paper.

"Excuse me, miss."

Faye raised her head. "Sorry, I was miles away."

"The man you were with outside, was that Samuel Delaney?" the woman behind the bar asked, wiping a glass with a cloth.

"It was Samuel Walsh. Do you know him?" Faye questioned, her forehead creasing.

"Yeah, I know him but his name isn't Walsh. He is a Delaney."

"Maybe he is a different Samuel then."

"Sweetie, I am telling you, that face is etched on my memory. That was Samuel Delaney, Angela Delaney's son."

"Can I ask how you know him?"

"I think you should ask Samuel that, but he was a regular here when the town was small. Everyone knew everyone's business back then."

"Well, thank you for the sandwich but I'd better head off," Faye said, her stomach twisting at the thought of another side to Samuel that she knew nothing about.

"I hope I didn't put you off. You have left half of it on the plate."

"No, no, I just don't have much of an appetite. Do you have a map of the town so I can find my way back?" Faye asked, pushing the plate away and trying not to look intimidated by the woman.

"There is one at the reception desk. Is there anything you are looking for? I might be able to guide you in the right direction."

"I'll be fine. Oddly, I like to find out about new places by myself. Thank you for the food." Getting up from her stool, Faye began to leave, but the bar lady called her back.

"Sorry, sweetie, but you left your jacket at the bar."

Faye tried to think of a quick excuse not to go back into the bar. "Oh, thanks. I probably won't need it."

"This is Ireland. You'll need it," the woman answered, holding the jacket out in her hand and waiting for Faye to take it from her.

Relieved she didn't have to go back inside but fuming inside knowing the woman was right, she took it from her with a strained smile.

Unfolding the map, Faye spread it out on one of the outside tables. The route suggested for the food festival

162

began only a few feet from where she stood. Thinking she would start there and walk around before heading back, she looked back at the front of the flyer.

In bold type, the dates of the food festival were spread over the page. The event didn't start until the following day and spanned the weekend until Monday morning. The activities were listed for each day starting at ten in the morning. Faye deposited the map in her bag, a little disappointed, then started her walk into the small town.

It took a few minutes for Faye to get her bearings amongst the crowds of people in the town. Arriving at the main street, she stopped outside a quaint shop. Faye inhaled the aroma of mixed perfumes floating out of the door.

In the window, little houses were scattered with fairies in different dresses with wands. They hung from thin wire posed to look as though they were flying. Gold dust was sprinkled on the floor between the houses with footprints in it. Around the inside of the window, small white lights flickered on and off, bringing the whole display to life. Small black buckets sat by the door of each house, with lit wicks sticking out of the centres, giving off the aroma that had made Faye stop. She took a few photographs with her phone then squeezed through the slender door to enter the shop. She was instantly in awe.

Shelves on both sides were packed with handmade gifts – soaps that looked like cupcakes, candles in different shapes and sizes, jewellery made in pastel colours and fairies, lots and lots of fairies.

For a small shop, Faye felt lost in it. Her senses were heightened from all the fragrances hitting her. She stood in the centre, not sure what to smell first.

"Would you like any help?" A man came from the counter to assist her.

"There is so much here. I don't know where to start."

"Okay, close your eyes and when one of the scents makes your belly warm, that is the candle you need."

Faye closed her eyes, and a sweet aroma whiffed under her nose. Instantly, she shook her head. Much too sweet for her taste.

The next, she didn't know if she should poke her tongue out to lick. Caramel, definitely the odour of caramel. Although she liked it, it didn't make her belly warm.

Two more wafted under her nose, both equally enticing but not *the one*.

It started from her memory, taking her back to winter days – her hands wrapped around hot chocolate, sitting in front of the her grandmother's electric fire while the smell of baking came from the kitchen and the rain hammered on the window, trying to force its way in but failing. The warmth came from her belly, stirring until her eyes snapped open.

"Here is your candle Coilín."

The gentleman wrapped the candle in bubble wrap,

placed it in a brown paper bag and added a bow at the top to seal it.

"Does it have a name? A brand or something?" Faye asked, wanting to know where to buy more when she got home.

"Everything you see here, we make. The candle that chose you is called Grandma's Cottage."

When she left the shop with a bag full of items, the sun had retreated and left a chill in the air. Although the street seemed busy, Faye felt relaxed walking amongst the visitors. Her bags swung from the fold at her elbow as she walked back towards The Huddle with her arms folded across her chest.

All of the seats outside were taken. Chatter floated through the air while the revellers enjoyed the last of the day. Faye walked through the reception and towards the bar, stopping dead at the threshold.

Her mouth gaped open, and she swore inwardly, trying to stop the tear hanging onto her eyelash for dear life from falling. Samuel was sitting on a wooden stool, propped up at the bar with his brogues resting on the spindles. Faye could feel heat travelling to her cheeks while pain formed in her stomach, a void where he should have been. She had no right to think that way. He didn't belong to her anymore. She had made that clear more than once.

He wasn't a broad man, but he had muscles that protruded through the dark grey t-shirt he wore. His thighs were solid. They had pinned Faye up against walls many times. She needed to block those memories out. She needed to swallow her pride and make her way over to him.

But her feet refused to move.

Samuel had company.

He was leaning on his elbows, resting his hand on his cheek, deep in conversation with the stranger who had served her earlier.

The woman smiled, her focus on the man – Faye's man – directly in front of her. Brushing her red curls away from her neck, the woman angled her head to one side. From where Faye was frozen, she could see the woman's eyes shining as she spoke to Samuel. Faye wished she had questioned the stranger more when she'd had the chance. She wanted to kick herself. The woman's hand stroked Samuel's bare arm, sending hot rage coursing through Faye's body.

She wanted to grab the woman's hair, twist it fiercely in her hand, and tell her to keep her claws out of her man. But how could she? Samuel had no commitments to her. They were no longer in a relationship. Faye had made it clear she'd only tagged along as a friend, but that didn't stop her blood from boiling. Her eyes felt like they were holding back a waterfall that needed to burst.

She needed to make a decision – either walk away, pretend she saw nothing and let them have their moment, or straighten her shoulders, hold her head up high and join them at the bar to show Samuel she could control her feelings.

She never had to make the choice. A group of rowdy men entered the bar, knocking Faye in their hurry, and headed straight for the bar, demanding drinks.

At the commotion, Samuel turned around and his eyes instantly met Faye's. She could feel her face redden, annoyed at the men and sickened that she looked clumsy in front of Samuel's friend.

The woman behind the bar snatched her hand away from Samuel's and began wiping the counter. Faye bent down and gathered her bags, hoping that the glass around her cottage candle hadn't broken. The tear she had fought so long to hold back, fell.

"Hey, let me help you with those." Crouching down, Samuel helped to retrieve her shopping from the floor.

"It's fine. I've got it." She snatched the last few bits and shoved them into the brown paper bag.

"Here, let me carry it."

"I'm quite capable, Sam. I just got knocked."

Not taking no for an answer, Samuel took the remaining bags and stomped towards the sitting area.

Faye followed. She knew Samuel well enough to know when he wanted to avoid something. He stood by a set of chairs, placing the bags next to one.

"Sit. You must be wrecked after all that walking."

"I don't want to sit, Sam. I want a drink."

"I will get one for you."

"Why can't we both go back in?"

"It is busy in there now."

"So? We can drink outside."

"It will be quicker if I just go. We wouldn't want you to be trampled, would we?"

Faye knew it was useless trying to argue with him. He didn't want her going in there and she knew why.

And that hurt her more.

He was holding back more details of his life from her.

The eggshells she'd walked on since the arrival of the dreaded letter had been the reason for the break-up text she'd sent him. She hadn't been able to face him. He had a way with words that clouded her thoughts. He would have changed her mind then left her in the dark again, refusing to tell her about what troubled him. It frustrated her, and here he was doing it again.

Faye sat on the low couch, waiting. With every minute Samuel took, Faye visualised him ordering the drinks at the bar with the scarlet woman smiling at him, touching him, planting a kiss on his cheek, threading her fingers where Faye's should have been. The clock over the reception desk ticked away slowly, laughing at her with each sweep of the hand.

Twenty slow, agonising, lonely minutes passed before Samuel returned and placed the drinks on the table. Faye's hands trembled in her lap in anger, her mouth pursed together and her face flushed waiting for Samuel to sit down.

"That took a long time," Faye's words hung sarcastically in the air, as one of her eyebrows rose.

"You saw how busy it was in there. I had to wait my turn."

"Really? Over twenty minutes waiting your turn? Did the redhead have to squeeze lemons for the mixer or does she always look that sour?"

"If you have something to say, Faye, then say it. Don't hold back."

"Fuck you, Samuel." Fuming, Faye grabbed her bags from under the table, and stormed off towards her room, she left Samuel to have his drink alone. When she got to her room, though, her first thought was that now he had free rein to go back to that woman, and she wanted to cry. Cry for pain that he had caused her, cry for catering to his whims and going there with him in the first place, and cry for the old Samuel she'd known before the letter had arrived, when he'd loved her.

Falling onto the bed, she let her feelings pour out with her tears, and eventually, her damp eyes succumbed to sleep.

A light tap on the door startled her awake.

She sat up in the bed, her clothes ruffled from sleep. She waited, tilting her head in the direction of the door.

Knuckles tapped on the door again, this time, a little louder. Faye got up from the bed and stood behind the door, her ear pressed against the barrier between her and whoever stood on the other side.

There were three more hard knocks.

Rubbing the sleep from her eyes, Faye wanted nothing more than to crawl back into bed and hide under the covers. Knowing the only way that could happen was to stop the culprit from knocking, she slowly opened the door. Peeking through the small opening she saw Samuel leaning against the frame, his head hanging low.

"What the fuck do you want, Samuel?" she asked croakily.

Samuel looked up from the floor, pain etched on his face. "I need to come in, Faye."

"Go back to bed. You're not welcome here." She tried to close the door, but Samuel wedged his foot in the gap to stop it.

"I can't."

"Why? Can you not get rid of the red in your bed?"

"What are you talking about?"

"The woman at the bar who enjoyed your company so much. Took her back to your room, did you?"

"For fuck's sake, what kind of friend do you take me for?"

"An arsehole of a friend."

Samuel licked his thin lips, piercing Faye with his blue

eyes.

"Faye, you are my world. I would never do anything to hurt you. Please, just let me in."

Faye blinked a few times at his confession, her eyes on Samuel's for the first time since opening the door. He looked like shit with his dishevelled curls stuck to his forehead and bristles on his chin that needed trimming. He looked like a man who hadn't slept in a long time. Faye couldn't help but tell him that, in those exact words. His mouth turned up at the edges, but the smile never reached his eyes.

"I *haven't* slept for a long time," he confessed, breaking a piece of Faye's heart.

Standing back to open the door wider, she allowed Samuel to enter the room. The life seemed to drain from his body with each step. Expelling the air from his chest, he sat on the edge of the bed and rubbed an unseen crease from the cover. "I thought I woke you."

"You did. I fell asleep on the covers."

"Oh, that would make more sense."

Faye closed the door then moved to the only chair in the room, pulling on the hoodie she had left on it. Sitting opposite Samuel, she pulled her knees up and cradled her arms around them.

"What do you want, Samuel?"

"I couldn't sleep," he said, speaking to his hands on his lap rather than to Faye directly. "I, well, I have been having those, you know, those disturbing dreams."

"Did you have one just now?"

"Yeah."

"Do you have the same dream or different ones?"

Faye had never heard Samuel open up about his night terrors. She had always wanted him to, begged him even, but he'd always refused.

The one she'd witnessed had frightened her, but Samuel had left the following day to come to Ireland.

"Do you want to tell me what the dreams are about? It might help."

"Seriously, I don't think that would help. I really thought coming here last month would put an end to them, but it didn't."

"Why did you have to come here? You packed your bags and ran. I wanted to talk, needed you to talk, but you shut me out."

"Faye, please trust me when I say I can't tell you. Parts of my past are better off staying hidden. I don't want to even remember them."

"Samuel, look at me." Faye unravelled her legs and moved closer to feel the heat radiating from him, but all she felt was cold.

Rubbing his hands along his thighs, he lifted his head but didn't meet her eyes.

"Don't you think that if you told me or at least spoke to someone, your nightmares might go?"

"I am not going to lie on a couch while some shrink tells me I am going insane or blames my past for my behaviour now. All that stuff is shit."

"Don't you think you have answered your own question there? Maybe your past *is* the reason for your behaviour. Think about it."

"This is shit. You know that saying *let sleeping dogs lie*? Well, mine is one fucked up past that should be left alone. I should never have came here last month. I should have torn up that letter and the package with the key in and cut all ties. I didn't want to lose you."

Faye waited until Samuel stopped flexing his fists. He wanted to leave; she knew that much. Sitting with all that negativity circulating around his body made him tense, but a question still hung in the air.

"Who is that woman at the bar?"

Snapping his head towards her, he frowned. "What?"

"That woman, the redhead who seemed to like you a little too much – who is she?"

"Fuck." Samuel took in a deep breath, rubbing his hand over the mouth Faye had kissed too many times to count. "Fuck."

"I'm not going to go ballistic. I have no right to. We...well, we're not together, but I need to know. You looked very intimate and I'd rather know than not."

Samuel leaned forward, his knees almost touching Faye's. They didn't need to, though. She could feel the heat coming off him.

"She is just another part of my past. That's all she is and all she will ever be. I honestly didn't know she worked here. I thought she'd moved away from this dead end town years ago, but apparently not."

"So she is an ex?"

"Yeah, something like that."

"Two exes in one bar must have given your ego a bit of a boost."

"Faye, this is shit. She is the past, this shit town is the past, and if it weren't for that key and paperwork, I wouldn't be here now. But you? I never want you to be my past. I want you now, I wanted you last week, and I wanted you last month. I asked you here with me because I knew I wouldn't have the strength to do this on my own."

Reaching over, Samuel laid his warm hands on Faye's thighs. The denim of her jeans protected her from the burn she would have felt, but nothing protected her from another piece of her heart slithering off and falling with the others that he had broken along the way.

Lost pieces.

Frayed, broken pieces.

She folded her arms, unable to trust herself not to wrap her hands around his.

"Okay then, tell me, why did you come here by yourself before?"

"It's complicated."

"I'm not going anywhere, so talk."

"Will you lay on the bed with me and then I'll talk?"

"Are you nuts?"

"I need to hold you. I promise I won't try anything."

"Your promises aren't that trustworthy, Samuel."

"This time, it is."

Faye's body moved before her brain could argue with her. She was conflicted between doing what she felt she should and what he needed. The conflict became a battle with each movement she took to close the gap between them.

Her body felt exhausted, her senses on overload. Seeing Samuel not looking his usual strong self, weighed on her. She missed being close to him, missed how it felt having him pressed against her body, and right now, whether right or wrong, she had more to gain than him.

Taking her hand, he guided her to the bed, keeping his eyes firmly on hers. She waited for him to slide to the middle of the bed, then, without making eye contact, she lay against his front, her back to him. Samuel's free arm encased her, pulling her towards him, leaving no gap between the two of them. He breathed her in and closed his eyes.

Silence fell comfortably between them. Faye started to drown in the comfort of his embrace, falling into a zone of remembrance.

"When that letter arrived, it brought back my past. I

wanted to rip the fucking thing up into little pieces and post it back. We were good before that letter, weren't we?"

His words pulled Faye back to where they were. She nodded her head to agree, not wanting to speak in case she broke the spell that had Samuel opening up.

"That's what I should have done, but I didn't. I know I pushed you away. I had to. My head filled up with things that should be illegal. I couldn't have you near me. I wanted to protect you. That is why I came over here. I had to put an end to all of this. I hoped that would be enough to put my life back on track. But it didn't end up like that. Your text broke me."

Faye's body tensed. The text had broken her, too, but she said nothing.

Not yet.

She shifted slightly from his hold to give herself the space she craved in that moment of guilt, but he pulled her back, holding her tighter.

"I don't blame you for wanting to move on. I'm not exactly Mr. Fun-To-Be-Around lately. I get it, Faye. I really do. You're gorgeous, but I'm not worthy. This key has thrown me, just like the letter, and honestly, I just want the whole thing to be over."

The last few words hung in the air. He wanted it all to be over... Whether he meant the business with the key or her, she couldn't decipher. One thing she did know, he had given no answers to why things changed.

Yes, she knew it had something to do with the letter.

Yes, she knew it had something to do with Ireland, but what?

"You haven't told me anything. I have no idea why you had to be here last time, what's written in the letter or even who wrote it. You are confusing me more than helping me understand."

"This isn't easy for me."

"And you think this is easy for me?"

"There are things about my past that wouldn't be right for you to know."

"Meaning what? Did something happen to you?" Turning from her side, she yearned to see his face, to see what he wasn't saying, but he stopped her, holding her securely to his front.

"Let's just say it wasn't exactly an ideal upbringing."

"What is an ideal upbringing nowadays? Crikey, Sam, this world is so fucked up on so many different levels that no one knows what is normal anymore. What is wrong for some is right for others. That, I guess, is what makes the world amazing and terrifying at the same time."

Samuel moved the hand that was propping him up and placed it between them, resting his head down on the pillow. Faye could feel his hot breath on her neck making her skin prickle.

"You're right, but my upbringing was definitely wrong."

"Do you want to talk about it?"

"No."

"How are you going to let me in if you don't tell me what all this is about?"

"It isn't that easy. When I left you today, I did it for two reasons. One ~ I knew you wanted to see what the shops had to offer, which gave me the opportunity to visit my aunt. We didn't exactly part on good terms the last time I left. Tomorrow, I'm taking you to see the house that I have the key for. I didn't want you to hear cross words from her if I hadn't cleared the air today. Two ~ I didn't want anyone to recognise me in town."

"Oh, why the bad terms?"

"History, not doing something my aunt wanted."

"It seems like you are good at pissing people off. So what if people recognise you in the town?"

"Don't you get it? I don't want to be recognised. I don't even want to be here. This town is full of small-minded people who love to gossip. I don't need that distraction right now."

"What about your lady friend at the bar? She knew you alright."

"That shouldn't have happened."

"But she is still living here even though you think this town is bad?"

"Life changes, I guess. Different priorities take over."

"Did you even ask her?"

"I didn't have to. Molly O'Brien talks too much."

"Samuel, will you do me just one thing while we are here?"

"Anything."

"Will you not flirt with your past in front of me? At least wait until I have gone to bed."

"You have my word, and for the record, I wasn't flirting. That was the last thought in my head."

Faye yawned and closed her eyes. The morning wanted to begin, but she wasn't ready for it. No matter how much she tried to fight it, sleep was closing in fast.

"Tell me one thing before I fall asleep. Where is your mother now?"

"Dead. Cold on a slab in the hospital."

Twenty Two

The morning sun woke Samuel, the nightmares having given him a break for one night. He stretched his aching arms above his head and rolled from his back to find an empty space beside him. Sitting up, still in his clothes, he swore at himself for not having the balls to tell Faye everything. The words had been on the tip of his tongue, and yet they got stuck in his throat when he wanted to spit them out. Now Faye would think he was as weak as water, fobbing her off with nothing concrete again.

He did a quick scan of the room to check if her bag and her belongings were still there, that she hadn't left and run like he'd wanted to the previous night. Faye had more strength than he did. He hadn't even been able to look at her when he'd eventually spoke. Seeing pity etched on her delicate face would have destroyed him. He hadn't thought she would agree to lie on the bed with him, but it had made what he did manage to say come out easier. Samuel felt selfish for needing Faye with him to feed off her strength.

He'd had to clear the thoughts bombarding his brain when he pulled her into him. A simple touch in the right place could have led them down the wrong path, but he'd promised her. He couldn't go back on his word, no matter how much it killed him.

Faye's hoodie occupied the chair she'd sat on last night and her bags were still in the corner of the room. Content she hadn't run, he retrieved his socks and put them on.

A rush of water could be heard from the bathroom. Relieved Faye hadn't abandoned the room altogether, he scribbled on the guest notepaper to let her know he was doing the same in his room and would come back to her in thirty minutes. Leaving the note propped up on the bed he snuck out.

With Faye in the passenger seat, Samuel pulled out of The Huddle's car park and made his way out of town to the cottage that now belonged to him. Neither mentioned the conversation the previous night or why they hadn't attended breakfast in the dining room. When the car arrived outside a whitewashed house surrounded by fields, they were welcomed by the smell of bacon and sausages wafting through the air.

Samuel opened the car door for Faye and smiled softly at her. She nodded a silent thank you.

"Home sweet home," he said, referring to the dormer house.

"Wow, the house is simply breathtaking, Samuel."

"It's not mine, so don't get too excited."

Leading Faye in through the open door, Samuel guided her to the large family kitchen past the *good* front room where his aunt had confronted him the previous day with a few home truths that he deserved. He'd stood his ground, though, fought his case and won.

"Deirdre?" Calling his aunt nervously, he hovered at the table, not willing to sit until his aunt said.

Turning away from the cooker with a spatula in her hand, Deirdre's eyes darted from Samuel to Faye and back again.

"Aunty Deirdre, this is Faye, my closest friend. I explained to you yesterday." Faye shot him a look and he shrugged his shoulders.

Deirdre rubbed the palms of her hands down her apron then held out her hand and stepped closer to Faye.

"Hello, my dear. I have heard a lot about you, and not just yesterday. Come in, sit down, don't want the house to look dirty."

Samuel pulled out a chair at the table and offered it to Faye, taking a seat next to her.

"It is an old saying if someone stands at the door for too long. Not sure where it came from but Aunt Deirdre uses it often," Samuel explained while his aunt put the kettle on the range.

"Oh, I was wondering how I was making the house

look dirty," Faye whispered back, not wanting to offend his aunt.

"Samuel, ye can make the pot of tea for your guest. Dee has gone out for a walk up the town with Tadgh to see the stalls. I hope you will at least take Faye to see what good food this town is known for while you are here."

"Maybe tomorrow," Samuel answered, jumping up on his aunt's instructions and throwing two teabags into the teapot while he waited for the water to boil.

"When was the last time you made a pot of tea?" Deirdre asked him, taking the teabags out again with a huff. "Warm the pot up first, lad and then put in the bags. That's the problem with city folk. It's all convenience coffee cups. I bet neither of you has had a proper breakfast. No, I guess not," Deirdre answered, shaking her head before Samuel could open his mouth.

Taking out a couple of plates from the cupboard, Deirdre stacked up sausages, bacon, black and white pudding with beans and placed the plates on the table when the kettle whistled.

Samuel made the tea the way he had been taught by Deirdre many years ago, knowing she had her eye on him. When he had finished, she smiled warmly, and Samuel's heart softened to see her proud of the teaching.

The three of them sat in silence while they filled their stomachs and drank the tea.

Faye placed her knife and fork on her plate and filled

her mug. "Thank you so much for the breakfast, Mrs. Walsh. I don't think I can move from this table I am so full."

"You're welcome, dearie. It is nice to cook for someone who likes good food. Samuel, you can clean up the plates and put them in the dishwasher. I am going to take Faye outside."

"Outside? Why?" Panic beat through his veins.

"Because things have to be said and I am sure you didn't say them."

"Oh fuck, Deirdre, don't do this."

"Samuel Delaney, you curse in this house again and I swear there will be no coming back."

Faye had never seen Samuel back down from anyone until that moment. Scraping his chair along the tiled floor, he pushed it back with force, fuming and red faced. Deirdre quietly got up and took off her apron, waited for Faye to join her, and they both left Samuel standing with his back to them with his shoulders hunched over the sink.

Samuel leaned against the white Belfast sink and watched Faye standing nervously in the middle of the patio. It wasn't often he saw her so unsure and he hoped his aunt didn't say something she would regret. Faye didn't need to know all the details, and he knew it would change everything if she did.

If he sat at the kitchen table, he would be able to watch their every move, but he wouldn't give his aunt the satisfaction. Instead, he opened the window slightly and waited for them to be seated, overlooking the green fields. In the distance, he could hear sheep bleating in the cool breeze, and then he heard Faye's soft voice speaking to his aunt.

"Mrs. Walsh, I think it would be better if I heard this from Samuel. It is his story to tell."

Samuel smiled, pleased that Faye had the courage to speak her mind to his aunt.

"I wanted to make him stew, Faye. He is a little boy lost in an adult body and needs a good kick up the behind."

"Oh, so you're not going talk about his past?"

"It isn't mine to tell, but I will tell ye this. That boy in there needs to sort out his life and fast. I brought you out here because from what I have heard about you through the years, you are his strength. He doesn't know it yet, but the day you walked into his life, when he left here, happened to be the day he started living again. You did that, no one else. I wanted to thank you for being there when I wasn't."

"Oh, but, Mrs. Walsh..."

"Call me Deirdre. Mrs. Walsh makes me sound like my mother."

"Deirdre... Inside you called him Samuel Delaney. I have only known him as Samuel Walsh."

"Is that right? Well, at least he took part of us with him when he left. Walsh, as ye now know, is my husband's family name. Delaney is Samuel's mother's maiden name and mine, too. He must have dropped it when he moved over. Well, I'll be dammed."

Samuel moved away from the window. He had heard enough to know his aunt's tongue was staying firmly away from his tale, not giving up the secrets her sister kept.

Filling a mug with freshly made coffee from the machine, he opened the sliding door to the patio and stepped outside, breathing in the fresh, clean air.

"We are going to look in the cottage, Deirdre. Do you want to come?"

"No, Samuel, it is yours to delve into. I don't need to be there."

"Well, in that case, Faye, are you ready to go or are you still chatting?" Samuel tipped his head back to finish the dregs of the coffee he desperately needed to fill a void, before placing the mug on the table.

Before Faye could answer, Samuel had already started to make his way through the trodden down grass to the empty cottage. As she quickened her step to catch him up, Samuel waited at the end of the small steps to guide her.

"This place is beautiful, Samuel. I cannot believe you haven't been back here for so long."

"The view is deceptive. It diverts your attention away from other things."

"Really? Like what?"

Faye stood at the first step, holding on to Samuel's fingers before taking another. Samuel looked at how beautiful she was. The sun shone around her head like a halo, and he wished he could confess the secrets that were still fresh in his mind, but then her innocence would be broken. The smile she gave only to him would be swapped for sympathy and that glow would vanish. He couldn't do that to her.

"Come on, Faye. We can't view the house unless we go inside." Gently, he pulled her hand to make her move from her spot and she sidestepped down the other overgrown steps.

"This might be an obvious question, but why are there steps between your aunt's place and here?"

"Well, this cottage belonged to the Delaney family years ago along with the farm. My aunt and her siblings lived here with my grandparents, helping with the farm and such. When Deirdre got married, some of the land and the farm passed over to her and she built the house. My Uncle Seamus continued living here with his parents until they passed away. He helped out on the farm until his death."

"Shouldn't the son get the farm, though?"

"Ideally, yes, but my aunt is the eldest and you know what? I've never questioned it."

"What about the other sibling?"

"Moved into town at a young age."

"Didn't work on the farm then?"

"Nope."

Samuel took the key out of his back pocket, wanting to enter the cottage and steer away from questions he didn't know the answers to. It took a few tries before the door would unlock, years of rust fighting with the key. Putting his shoulder against the wooden door, he pushed hard to dislodge the rusty hinges. With a creek, the door opened to expose the dusty interior.

"Wow, this is some place," Faye exclaimed, leaving her footprints in the dust on the floor as she walked in.

"It looks smaller than I remember."

"Well, you aren't exactly a teenager now, are you?"

"True, every part of me has grown."

"Samuel!"

Samuel grinned, making his way through the small sitting area to the kitchen at the back of the building. The cottage looked very much like it had when his uncle had lived there. After his death, the door must have been shut and the key turned in the lock. It looked as though no one had set foot inside since. He wondered if Deirdre knew then that the place had been left to her sister and that was why she walked away from the property.

"So, is this yours now? Did you sign the papers for the change of deeds yesterday?" Faye asked, joining Samuel at the kitchen in the back of the small property.

"It will have to go through probate first. That takes time, but I am sure no one will mind if it is cleaned up while the paperwork is sorted."

"I thought all you had to do was sign for it. That's why we came, isn't it? Are you okay to accept this even though you're not exactly over the moon with who left it to you?"

Samuel took his time to answer. If his mother had lived in the house after he was born, if his memories of the cottage had included her, then he would rather have burned the place down, but they didn't.

He had used to sit at the table, his legs dangling from the chair while his uncle gave him tea from a chipped tea cup with a slice of bread and jam. Those were his memories. This was a place he had escaped from his mother to on the rare occasions Deirdre persuaded her to allow him out. Then later, when he'd moved into his aunt's for good, the cottage had become his haven.

"I thought that was all I had to do, but no. As for accepting it, her name may be on the deeds, but this place never truly belonged to her."

"Have you thought about what you want to do with it now?"

Samuel shrugged his shoulders. On the journey over he'd had a plan. He would hand the key to Dee to do with as she pleased. Then he would have been free to go back to his bar and the door would have been truly closed to any return. However, after entering the cottage, smelling the dusty old place and remembering himself there in happier times, he wasn't so sure.

"I'm not going to rush into anything. I'll give it a little clean and then think about it back home."

"So you're not going to give up the bar and move

here?"

"Here? Did the dust make you light-headed?"

"It was just a question, Samuel."

"I'm going to get some black bags from Deirdre. If we clear out the kitchen to start with, that should do for now. You don't mind, do you?"

"What? Being brought over to Ireland to clean and missing out on a day walking around a food festival in the sun? No, I don't mind at all," Faye remarked sarcastically.

"Good. I won't be long."

Samuel moved a broken chair and rubble from the back door. It opened inward, allowing light to flood inside. Leaving Faye standing at the edge of the room, he paused, letting the country morning air fill his lungs and waiting for his head to clear. Having Faye in the cottage felt strange to him, like she didn't belong. She looked out of place.

As his feet travelled over the steps back to Deirdre's, he hoped it was only the dirt making him think that way.

Twenty Three

The grey dust clung to Samuel and Faye's clothes while they removed years of neglect. Both tried brushing the particles off, but they were too stubborn to move. Nothing escaped the veil of grey – every corner, every cupboard, anything that had a surface, a platform, a function once in its lifetime was coated in it. The kitchen, although not big, had room enough for a four seated table. One of the chairs was still pulled out like someone had left for a few minutes but never returned.

Ten black bags stuffed to the brim with everything that could be removed were lined up outside the back door. Samuel leaned on a sweeping brush, his hair coated white, his face ashen. Wiping the dust away from his lips, his focus drank in Faye as she fought to remove the dirt clinging to her hair. To him, she looked perfect – too perfect for the broken world he came from.

"You're going to need a shower before dinner." He swallowed, not adding that he would wash her clean, rub the soap delicately over her body, and sink his aching cock into her.

"You don't say. You're not much different. It suits you."

"Ha! I'm sure I have a few greys somewhere up there already."

"Are we done here for the day? I ache all over." Her words made his jeans tighten in the wrong place. He wanted to make her ache, not the work they had managed to do in the last few hours, and a jealous pain hit his chest.

"Yeah, and I am starving. The room looks a bit more spacious now, though," Samuel stated, viewing the work they had achieved through the open door.

Faye stretched her arms above her head, leaning back to ease her muscles. "Are we coming back again tomorrow?"

"I will. You can spend the day walking around the town. I'll ask Dee to go with you if you want company."

"No, it's fine. I quite liked going on my own yesterday."

"Then that's settled. Right, give me a minute to shut the back door and we can get back to the hotel."

"Are we saying goodbye to Deirdre first?"

"Best to, unless you want the silent treatment the next time we return."

"I think I am used to the silent treatment, don't you?"

Samuel shook his head. More than just his cock

deflated at that remark. Without saying another word, he waited outside the cottage for Faye to join him, closing the door behind her.

"Won't you need to lock up the house?" Faye asked, noticing there was no keyhole.

"It will be fine for the night. There's nothing in there worth taking anyway," Samuel replied, giving the door a final push to wedge it in the worn-out frame.

Deirdre stood at the entrance of her house. Samuel and Faye had said their goodbyes and Samuel had explained that he would be back early in the morning, on his own this time. His aunt had fussed over the state of them both, brushing their clothes down with a damp cloth and giving out to Samuel for making Faye's first visit tiresome. He'd kissed her goodbye and waved to her tired but content face as he drove out of the driveway, down the boreen and back to the main road.

He knew the moment they walked into the reception area that the atmosphere had changed in The Huddle. The place had been converted into a noisy, overflowing pub, all things Samuel did not need right then. Back at his own bar, he loved those kinds of evenings. The tills would be ringing and the punters would be many, but here in ShanInis, he didn't need the disturbance.

"I'm going straight to my room for a shower. Come by

in twenty minutes for dinner," Samuel said to Faye as they both walked towards the stairs.

"I might eat in the bar later. I'll meet you there if you want?"

"Did you not see how busy it is in there?"

"Yeah, that's why we should go in. I'd love to hear traditional music."

"I'd rather eat in my room with you than sit in there."

"Well, you know what, Samuel? Sit in your room. If you want to eat with me, I'll be down here."

She didn't wait for his answer. She just walked past him, leaving him on the stairs much to his frustration.

Twenty-two minutes later, Samuel paced his room, checking his watch every few seconds. He had showered quickly, dressed and waited, but deep down he knew she wasn't going to show. He hoped she wouldn't push him into making a choice he didn't want to make. The urge to use his faithful string had faded after the comment she'd made at the cottage. It had felt like a slap on the face, hitting him with the reality of the behaviour she had to endure.

Sitting downstairs in the crowded room with music vibrating off the walls didn't appeal to him. He didn't want his evening to end that way. A blinding headache would turn him into a pissed off Samuel. His stomach argued with him. He needed to stop being a pussy and make a decision. Picking up the phone in the room, he made the choice to call for room service.

He tried sitting down on the edge of the bed to wait, but that only made his legs restless. He should have ordered a light snack instead of listening to his hunger. He'd ordered the full works, and now he realised that would take longer to cook.

Checking his watch one more time, he finally made for the door and took large strides down to the bar where the music was coming from. With every stomp, he argued with his stubborn self. Go back to the room or give in to Faye. His feet made the choice for him.

He stood in the doorway scanning over the heads of all the people swinging and clapping to the music until he spotted Faye. There she sat, her hand midway to her ruby lips with a glass of the black stuff. He didn't want to move until he saw her take a mouthful, leaving the white line on her upper lip. The thought made his mouth curve slightly until the man next to her moved in close to talk into her ear. She nodded and gave a relaxed smile in response, making Samuel lean back onto the doorframe for support.

He hadn't seen that look for a long time. The urge to go over there and pull her out of her seat before knocking the lights out of the man was overwhelming. All his built-up tension could be resolved in one punch, and that man, with each breath he took beside her, came close to being on the receiving end.

Samuel took a step forward, his eyes pinned on them both as the room disappeared around him.

Faye rested her drink on the table. The man beside her touched her lip to smudge away the white foam left behind, and Samuel's rage grew. The music changed to an upbeat jig, bringing many people to their feet around him.

For a while, his vision blurred with the crowds of dancers. Samuel pushed away a couple in high spirits. They laughed as they tried to grab his arm and get him to join them. He spotted Faye standing up and allowing the man to lead her towards the dance floor. Neither noticed the fury in the look he shot at them.

Clenching his fist, he geared up to make contact with the intruder.

"Well hello, handsome. I knew you couldn't avoid me."

"Get out of my way, Molly," Samuel snarled at the woman who had stolen his heart years ago as she blocked his view.

"Samuel Delaney, are you not going to dance with me?" Molly pulled at his sleeve to coax him.

Samuel grabbed her arm and brought her close to his side.

"You know full well I don't dance," he whispered forcefully in her ear.

"You don't have to be so rough. What happened to you?"

"Shit happened, girl. Shit happened."

"You're hurting my arm. Please let me go."

Samuel looked down to where his hand was clasping her bare arm, letting go quickly. His fingerprints had left marks behind.

"Seriously, Sam, England hasn't done you any good."

"Who's that man over there, the one with Faye?" Samuel asked his focus back to where Faye and the man were now dancing and linking arms with the others.

"Come over to the bar. We are in the way here," Molly replied when yet another couple pushed past them.

"Will you tell me then?" His voice was pleading, but he didn't care. He had to know.

"Yes, yes, for feck's sake just move out of the way." Molly grabbed Samuel's arm to steer him towards the bar. Faye disappeared amongst the crowd again, making his temper rise.

"Here, I'll get you a drink while the bar is quiet. Sit your ass down on that stool where I can see you," Molly ordered, going behind the bar and pouring a double whiskey.

"Swig that back and take that shit look off your face. You will scare the punters away."

Samuel took the drink and poured it down the back of his throat, needing the sting to reach his gut.

"Why are you still here anyway? You should be living the high life in Dublin or somewhere," Samuel asked, lifting his empty glass for a refill.

Taking the tumbler, Molly replaced the liquid and slid

the glass back to him. Leaning over the bar, with the beat of the music still going strong, Molly licked her lips, making her red lipstick shine.

"I told you yesterday – circumstances keep me here. Anyway, there is nothing wrong with working for my parents. I enjoy being here and I'm damn glad I am now, or I would have missed bumping into you."

"Yeah, but you didn't tell me the real reason keeping you in this dead end town."

"Didn't I? I thought you wanted to know about that guy dancing with your woman."

"And I told you last night, she isn't my woman. She's just a good friend."

"Is that why you were getting ready to knock his lights out because he was with your *friend*?"

"He looked troublesome."

"You like her, don't you?" Molly asked, her mouth twisting. "I know that look all too well."

"That was years ago, Molly. How can you even remember?"

"I'll never forget that look you used to give me."

"So, who is he?" His tone grew sharper with her hesitance to tell him.

"The man? No idea. I guess he is here for the festival."

"Don't lie to me."

"I'm not. That's the truth. I've never seen him before."

Samuel finished his drink and slammed the glass

down, his temper pumping through the protruding veins in his hands.

"Thanks for the drink. Have a nice life," he said, sliding the empty glass towards her.

"Please stay here. Talk to me." Molly looked pained as she placed her hand over his.

"You're my past. This place holds too many memories and I don't need that right now. Let go."

"I need to talk to you, Sam. We need to talk."

"No, we don't, Moll. For fuck's sake don't cause a fucking scene." Samuel held her eyes with his, daring her to test his patience.

Reluctantly, her hand slid off his, and lowering her eyes, she quietly, almost in a whisper, spoke to him. At first, Samuel didn't hear her clearly, and when he turned his ear towards her, asking her to repeat it, she said it again.

"We have a child."

Twenty Four

Samuel couldn't remember clearly how he'd got back to his room, but blood was trickling from his knuckles. The four words Molly had spoken to him were going over and over in a loop in his head.

The food he'd ordered sat on a tray on the small round table, going cold, making the room smell of warm fries. Sitting on the bed, he held his fists closed, trying to stem the pain that shot through his fingers when he tried to flex them. He winced at the ache, cursing himself for acting so damn stupid.

The door of his room flew open and Faye marched in, her face crimson, her mouth opening and closing, spewing out words.

"You fucker! How dare you? Who do you think you are?" She stormed around the bed, her footing heavy and determined. Standing in front of Samuel, she grabbed his head with both of her hands and lowered herself to his level.

"You need serious help. You're lucky Dale isn't going to press charges. What the fuck did you think you were doing? How dare you spoil my evening? You don't own me."

She dropped his head and backed away from him, her hand covering her mouth in disgust. Samuel couldn't speak. He didn't know what to say to her. If his actions lately hadn't lost her then exposing what Molly had conjured up definitely would. He knew how she felt about kids. Any thread of forgiveness she might have offered would be useless once she knew.

He couldn't hide the revelation, though. Even if he got on the plane tonight, the problem would not go away. This child Molly thought was his might come knocking one day in the future. He wouldn't be able to sweep a child away the way he had his mother.

Faye moved towards the end of the bed, her arms folded tightly in front of her. He could hear the air rushing from her lungs as her body quivered from cold that didn't exist.

"Don't leave, Faye, please," Samuel pleaded. He couldn't watch her go not knowing if she would ever be back. He just couldn't.

Faye paused mid-step, keeping her eyes to the floor. "I'm not leaving." She swallowed, and Samuel watched the fight going through her head, a fight he had caused. "Your hands need cleaning up. I'm getting a towel from the bathroom to clean them."

Samuel got up from the bed and followed behind her, watching the way her body moved with each step. He thought how much he would miss holding on to her womanly hips when he pulled her to him. He knew every part of her body, inside and out, but he wanted to explore so much more.

He sat on the rim of the bath while Faye held the edge of the white towel under the running tap, squeezing the end to wring out the excess water. Standing between Samuel's open legs, she held his wrist and gently patted his knuckles to mop up the blood.

"That stings. Are you sure it is just water you have on it?"

"Don't be such a baby. You deserve any pain you get after what you did."

"What did I do?"

"You don't remember?" Faye asked in surprise.

"I remember being at the bar and then nothing until I got in here."

"You punched him. The poor guy didn't have a clue. You stormed up to us in the middle of a dance, pulled his arm away from my waist and knocked him out. You weren't satisfied with that, though. Then you had to lean over and punched him again with your other hand. That's fucked up stuff right there, Sam."

"Fuck, fuck, fuck."

"No kidding."

"Shit, did the whole place see?"

"Not only the whole place but people had their phones out videoing it, too."

"And he isn't going to press charges?"

"No, the redhead you were talking to last night had a word with him, offered his stay for free and said you'd had some kind of bad news that made you act that way."

"Did she now?"

"I don't like her, Sam."

Samuel held his breath. The opening to talk about the kid couldn't have come at a worse time. So he didn't say anything.

While Faye continued to clean up the red mess in silence, Samuel winced with each touch. Holding his hand more firmly, Faye continued to clean, ignoring his flinching. When she had wiped away the after effects of the evening, Faye used the other side of the towel to dry his hands, taking a step back when she had finished. Samuel tightened his thighs to stop her moving out of his legs. She held onto his arms so she didn't fall, and the tension built between them in the small room.

"Don't do this, Sam." Her voice was so quiet he barely heard.

"Do what?" Samuel asked, resting his hands on her legs to hold her in position.

"You know exactly what you are doing."

"I want you, Faye," he confessed, pinning her still with his blue eyes.

Samuel watched her mouth open, her tongue licking her bottom lip, and he moved his hands to her waist to pull her down towards him. Their lips hovered inches apart. He could taste her breath and wanted more. The ache he felt grew in his jeans and he wanted nothing more than to ease it. His head fought with him not to do this to her, but this only had one outcome – him sinking into her, allowing him a few moments of nothing else but their bodies entwined.

He carried Faye to the bedroom urgently, their mouths colliding in a frenzy. Pressing her up against the wall, he pulled the clothes from her body, leaving her standing in just her black underwear. Samuel lifted her bra from her breasts, taking an exposed nipple into his mouth like a starved babe.

He was hungry for her.

Starved to the point of consuming her.

Stripping out of his jeans and t-shirt, he quickly planted his lips back onto hers. He wanted to trace his tongue down her stomach until he was nuzzled between her legs, but he didn't want to leave her mouth again.

Faye's body shook beneath his touch as he slowly disposed of her underwear. Before he wrapped her legs around him, he paused, fixing his blue eyes onto her green and waiting.

"Don't stop, Sam. Don't overthink this."

"You sure? I'll stop. Even if it kills me, I'll stop."

"I want this. One moment. Please, Sam, take me."

Her words were his undoing. Using the wall as leverage, he guided his cock to her entrance. Enticing Faye to open wider, he pushed inside her dark void, rocking her into position. His frustration and anger all dissipated with each movement.

"Oh God, I missed you, Faye," Samuel confessed, leaning into her neck to leave his mark. The taste of salty skin drove him further inside as he sucked on her pink flesh.

"You're mine, always. Remember that."

Widening his stance, he dipped his hips, pushing further until Faye's moans grew louder. He wanted to last, to spend the whole night showing her how much he'd missed her, but his cock had other plans.

As he pinned her body with his and came inside her, the world stopped. They were the only two people who existed. Nothing else mattered. They connected. They were one.

Reluctantly, he disengaged, slipping his deflating cock from her warmth, and let her feet reach the floor. Keeping his damp body close to hers, he let his bruised hand find the spot between her folds.

Samuel's digit moved in a circular motion, the pad of his finger giving just the right amount of pressure. He listened to the way her breath hitched, to each moan leaving her clenched mouth, each muscle that tensed. Her body was talking to him without words.

Begging him for more.

Samuel increased his rhythm, pressing her naked body between the wall and his chest. He didn't stop, couldn't stop, until Faye cried out, her neck stretched back, her body giving itself over to him.

Her legs gave out from beneath her, and Samuel scooped her up, carried her to his bed and placed her down with care.

Lying down, he pulled the cover over them both, watching a tear escape from the corner of her eye.

"Hey, don't do that."

"This is wrong. We shouldn't have done that. Nothing has changed." Faye sobbed between words, not able to look at him.

"Don't overthink, you said. I wouldn't have gone further if you hadn't wanted me to."

"You're dangerous to be around, Sam. It can't happen again."

"We can sort this out. I don't like you upset."

"Can we? You have been so distant. Tonight in the bar should never have happened. Your signals are so mixed that they make my head spin. Push and pull all the time. Talk to me. Make me understand what is going on in that head of yours. I need answers."

"You'll hate me if I tell you."

"I hate you now."

Samuel held her head, made her look up at him. Her eyes were wet, puffy and sad.

"I never wanted to upset you, Faye, never. You are my everything."

"Then show me, trust me, Samuel. If you don't trust me with what is going on, we are nothing."

"Shit, Faye."

"Do you trust me?"

"You are the only person I have ever trusted."

"Then tell me what's going on. What was in the letter that started this rollercoaster of destruction?"

"I can't."

"Then we are done, Sam, seriously done."

Samuel leaned back to see the light in her eyes dim. He couldn't tell her everything about the letter and what his mother had put him through. He couldn't live with her reaction. He didn't want her out of his life. The uncertain hush grew, and he had no choice but to watch Faye leaving the bed, dressing and walking out of his room, not looking back.

The click of the door closing felt like a slap to the face. Kicking off the cover, he picked his clothes up off the floor and dressed in a hurry. Grabbing the tray from the table, he threw it across the room, narrowly avoiding the flat screen TV on the wall, and stormed out taking his car keys with him.

He wanted to follow Faye to her room and beg for forgiveness, but he had no right to. Instead, he took two steps at a time and stomped out of the front door.

He knew he shouldn't be driving, not after the double shot of whiskey he'd drunk earlier, but his rage clouded any reasonable thought. Starting the car, he put it into gear and revved the engine. As he began to let the handbrake off, the passenger door swung open. Sliding into the seat next to him, Molly pinned his stare until he shook his head and swore under his breath.

"Well, where are we going then?"

"We are not going anywhere. Get out, Molly."

"No, we have talking to do."

"A bit late now, isn't it?"

"I did want to tell you, but Da said no."

Samuel glared out into the dark, his hands clenched tight around the steering wheel, his grazed knuckles weeping.

"Put your seat belt on," he told her. Steering the car out of the car park, he sped onto the empty road, his wheels spinning off the gravel with his speed.

They sat in silence. Samuel took the car out of town and onto the winding roads of the cliff edge. Molly clung on to the door handle as he took the bends at a speed not meant for country roads. By the time Samuel turned the engine off, Molly could breathe again. Taking off his seatbelt now that they were in the car park, the closed coffee shop below them, Samuel turned in his seat towards her.

"Right, speak."

"Aren't you the demanding one?"

"No games, Moll, I'm not in the mood."

"I think we have passed the game stage, don't you?"

Samuel turned the key in the ignition, allowing the engine to fire back to life.

"What are you doing?"

"Leaving. I don't have time for this shit."

"Stop, Sam. I'm only messing with you. God, you are so uptight."

Samuel shook his head, turned the engine back off but kept his fingers tight around the steering wheel. He turned his head towards her, his eyes blazing.

"You left with a one-way ticket. I didn't know I was pregnant when you went," Molly confessed, her eyes starting to fill up at the memory.

"You had your future all planned out. Off to Dublin, a career, a future, why didn't you get rid of the baby and go?" he barked at her.

"Are you serious? Get rid of the baby? *Our* baby!"

"But look how you ended up, stuck in this town with no future."

"And you are asking why I didn't tell you before? Well, you have just answered for me, you arsehole."

"Well, what have you done since I have left? Changed

nappies and made bottles?"

"You're such a dick! You know nothing about me or our daughter."

"Daughter is it? Why doesn't that surprise me?"

"When did you become such a hard shell? Or was I too blind in my youth to see it?"

"Yep, this is me, the fucker with the hardest shell of them all."

Molly tried to open the door, but Samuel had locked it from his side of the car when he switched off the engine. Turning her back to him, she stared into the darkness. They could hear the waves hitting the rocks in the distance.

"I want to get out, Samuel."

"Yeah, I know, but it's dark and even though I am an arsehole, I am not letting you walk out there."

"You make me sick. Do you not even want to know what she looks like?"

"Do you expect me to be a part of her life? Or did you tell me for another reason?"

"That is up to you. Neither of us needs you."

"Why did you tell me then?" Samuel challenged her, needing to figure out her intentions.

"When I saw you," Molly whispered, her words crackling, "all we had come flooding back. I guess you could call it selective memory. All I saw were the good times we had, the youth I lost. Tonight, you looked so different, so sad. It just rolled off my tongue. I dreamed for years about the moment I'd tell you about her. My dreams never ended with you punching some poor innocent man out of anger. I would never have told you if I had known."

"And now I know I can't exactly unknow."

"Yeah, well, you can go back to the UK and we will head back to Dublin after the festival."

"Dublin? I thought you lived at the pub."

Molly moved to face him, her mouth pressed into a thin line. "You shouldn't have jumped to conclusions then, should you?"

"Do you have someone waiting for you there?"

"Are you asking if I'm available?"

If the handbrake and cup holder column between them had disappeared, Samuel's knee would have been touching Molly's. In the small, confined space she smelt different, not his. He had no room to feel jealous – grateful, yes, but not jealous of the plastic keeping their touch apart.

"Are you?" he asked, his eyebrow cocked.

"Feck off, Samuel. I wouldn't get back with you if you were the last man in Ireland."

"So all that crap in the bar was you being a tease?"

"By the look of ye this evening, I think you are in enough mess with one woman. I couldn't help but tease you. There is a man – a kind, amazing man who took my child and me into his world."

"I'm really pleased to hear that," he said, brushing away a droplet of sweat that was dripping down his face.

"What? That you are off the hook as daddy?"

"No, fuck. Shit, this is wrong. My fucking mouth spurts out stupid things before I can rein it in lately. I'm happy that you have found someone who loves you both. It is more then I would have given you."

"I know that, and when I told my parents of my plans to go to university in Dublin, they were very supportive. Niamh came with me and within a couple of years I met Steve and our lives became complete."

"But you didn't have any more kids with him?"

"That is none of your business."

"You're right, it's not. Does Niamh – beautiful name by the way – know about her father, about me?"

"She knows Steve as her father, but yes I have told her that her paternal parent was someone from my youth."

"Am I... God I never thought I would say this, but am I supposed to be in her life now? I honestly don't know how this is meant to play out."

"I don't know either. The ball is in your court. You need to work out if you want to be a part of her life. If not then walk away and say nothing. If you do then call me."

Samuel nodded his head in agreement and started up the car to make the journey back to the pub.

Could he be in his daughter's life?

Would Faye want him to?

Would Faye ever talk to him again if or when he told her?

No answers would come, only guilt, silence, and a ticking bomb getting ready to explode. He couldn't even be sure whether Faye would talk to him.

Entering the lobby, neither of them spoke, both caught up in their own heads. Soundlessly, they went their separate ways.

Samuel reached his room, greeted by the mess he'd left behind. He wanted to crawl into bed, pull the cover over him and inhale Faye's scent, but that would have to wait.

Cleaning the debris as much as he could, he left the tray outside the room. Not ready to climb into bed yet, he stood under the shower and let the water hammer his exhausted body, hoping that the fucked up man he had become would be washed down the drain. Once he was dry, he slid under the covers and wrapped himself up in the memories of Faye.

Sleep didn't come easily, but his nightmares did. His eyes stared up at the ceiling, his heart racing in his chest as though it was trying to break free, as mixed up thoughts rolled over and over in his head.

He needed Faye.

Twenty Five

By nine the next morning, Samuel had finished clearing the kitchen of the cottage the best he could and had moved on to the smaller of the bedrooms. All the windows were open wide, letting in a cool breeze along with the sound of sheep bleating outside. As a young boy, he had been forbidden to enter the room that belonged to Uncle Seamus, and Samuel felt awkward being in there now. *Stay away from that room*, his uncle had always said when he went past the door to go the bathroom. *Nothing in there to interest your little mind and hands.*

His imagination had led him to believe that whatever Seamus kept behind the door must have been a treasure trove. Looking around the room now, he could see that hardly anything occupied it after all. The double cast iron bed sat against the back wall with black paint flaking from the rails. Samuel instantly thought what a great frame it was to tie rope to. He smirked, thinking that maybe that was what his uncle had hidden in there all along – a woman tied to the bed, waiting for the annoying boy to leave so Seamus could have his wicked way with her.

Aside from the bed, there was only an old wooden wardrobe, a chair similar to the kitchen ones and a set of drawers. Beside the bed, boxes were stacked five high.

Curiosity got the better of Samuel and he picked up the top box, sat down on the lumpy mattress, brushed off the dust with his hand and took off the lid.

Paperwork was crammed inside, envelopes with dog-eared edges, stacks of receipts, all paid in cash. Samuel pulled the top few out to see what Seamus had bought. Most were for the farm – feed, new stock and parts for machinery, but amongst them, one stood out. The receipt looked different to the others. The heading stated the shop had nothing to do with farming or groceries. It was from a nursery shop. The receipt, handwritten, also paid in cash, and it was for a cot. Samuel checked the date, and although it had faded over time, he could see the year of his birth in the top right-hand corner.

Holding the receipt in his hand, he got up and walked over to the small square window. Twisting the handle to loosen it, he pushed it open and poked his head out, gasping in the fresh air.

His birth must have been a drain on the family thirty-three years ago when the small town had doubtless enjoyed the gossip of the local country girl growing bigger without a man to claim her. Looking out at the fields that had once belonged to the smallholding, he wondered for the first time how the Delaney's had coped with the stigma. It certainly hadn't split the family if his uncle had purchased his cot all those years ago.

Leaving the window open, Samuel put the faded piece of paper back where he'd found it and closed the lid before picking up the next box.

The next three boxes contained more receipts, his uncle's birth certificate and a driving licence, but no passport. He never remembered his uncle travelling so not finding a passport did not surprise him. He finally propped the final box on his thighs. It looked no different to the others he had looked through, except for the string tied around it to secure it closed.

The knot on the top was tight and difficult to open. He carried it to the kitchen to retrieve a knife from one of the drawers that had yet to be emptied. Sitting at the table, he slid the bread knife under the tight string and started to saw. It broke through the threads one by one until the twine broke. He removed it and cautiously opened the box, unsure of what he would find inside. Why would a box need to be sealed?

This time, there were no receipts or personal documents. The box was filled with photographs – pictures of the Delaney children growing up, the cottage in its full glory and his grandparents. They looked like happy times, working in the fields and sitting outside enjoying the summer months while the children played. One photograph, in particular, caught his attention. The woman staring back at him from the black and white square smiled and looked happier than he had ever seen her. Turning the picture, he noted the writing on the back – Angela, May, age fourteen. Resting the photo on the table, he picked up the next one and read the back – Angela, Oct, aged fifteen.

The two photographs were in total contrast to one another. One showed a very carefree and smiley young girl, but the other was a different story. Angela was sitting on the second step at the back of the cottage. Her dress had been pulled down over her knees, covering right down to her ankles, and her smile was long gone. Her eyes didn't look into the camera the way they had in the first picture but stared vacantly into the distance.

Her cheeks were puffy, her hair long and dishevelled.

Samuel had seen that look many times. Whatever had happened in those summer months had changed his mother. He left the two pictures side by side and dug through the box again.

None of the photos gave any inkling of what had happened to change his mother, although he didn't know what he thought he would find. Samuel tipped out the photos onto the table and spread them out to look at them. Stuck to the bottom of the box, he found an envelope, stained with age, with Seamus's name on it in neat handwriting. Samuel tried to take it out but it was stuck in place and the envelope ripped. Turning the box upside down, he used the bread knife to cut out the bottom, making it easier to slide out the letter without destroying the fragile paper.

Carefully unfolding it, he laid the paper on the table, not wanting his dirty fingers to smudge the writing on the page. The handwritten letter consisted of only a few lines. The writing looked shaky, and Samuel had to read the brown tinted paper several times for the words to sink in, his own hand shaking. When he finally sat back in the chair, he let his focus drift towards the back door to find he wasn't alone.

"Did you know?" he spat out, unable to believe what he had read.

"Yes," his aunt replied, unable to look directly at him.

"And everyone covered it up, like the good holy people you all claim to be?"

"Times were different back then, so yes, we had to."

"HAD TO?" he shouted, thumping his fists down in rage. "HAD TO COVER THIS SHIT UP, FOR WHO?"

"Calm down. This is rural Ireland we are talking about, not a city."

"All these years, all the trouble I ended up in and I thought I had problems, but it was all you lot. Each and every one of you made me this way, made *her* that way. You do realise how much my life was fecked up because of this."

"Samuel, please keep your voice down. Dee is in the

kitchen up at the house and you know how the sound travels."

"That's how you managed to end up with the farm, isn't it? Payment for keeping your mouth shut."

"Now that's enough. I am not standing here taking the blame for trying to do what we all agreed was right. Do ye hear me?"

"This is shit. I don't want this fucking house. It should be burnt down with everything inside."

Deirdre stomped into the kitchen, stood where Samuel had sat and raised her hand, slapping him across the face and leaving a red mark behind. Samuel glared at her. Only inches separated them. He was almost daring her to do it again, but this time, he would be ready for her. In all the time he'd lived under her roof, she had never raised a hand to him, even when he desperately deserved it.

"You need to wash your mouth out with soap. That kind of talk will get you nowhere." She quivered, waving her finger and not backing away from him. "Now I am telling ye this. Stop behaving like a spoiled child. You are going to sit there until I finish with you."

His aunt moved away from him, her body shaking. She wedged the back door closed then took a seat opposite Samuel. He wanted to get up and punch a wall, punch anything rather than stay sitting, but he felt like a teenager again, being reprimanded for his behaviour. Instead, he composed himself the best he could, straightened his back and linked his fingers to stop them from balling into fists. He would give her a couple of minutes to explain; after that he was leaving.

"Go on then. I am all ears."

His aunt took in a breath, pursed her lips together then lowered her voice. What she wanted to confess was for his ears only and not the walls of the house. The cottage had seen and heard more than it should have in the years it had been occupied.

"It started when your mother turned thirteen. Her body turned into a woman's nearly overnight. One minute she was our baby sister, the next a full figured woman. She started to attract the boys in the town, which caused our father to be outraged on more than one occasion. I had already met Thomas and we started to court. Seamus hadn't left home. He spent most of his days in the fields helping Daddy." The words flowed out at speed, rushing to tell the tale hidden by the Delaney family for so long. Samuel could see from his aunt's restless fingers that what she confessed made her uncomfortable.

"By the time school had finished for the summer, all Angela wanted to do was spend time in the village, hanging around the boys, causing mayhem at home. One day after her fifteenth birthday, my mother had had enough after returning with some messages. She told Seamus to go to find her and bring her home.

"The sun had begun to set by the time his car pulled

up in the drive." Deirdre stared blankly at nothing, her voice quieter now. "She didn't say anything when she tramped through the house to the bedroom we shared at the back. Her face showed it all, though." Like a spell had been cast, Deidre shook away the vision playing in her mind and focused back on her hands. "Mammy was sitting at the table and never raised her voice. She drunk her tea and ate her slice of buttered bread, not reacting to the door slamming or Seamus leaving the house to stay in the barn. Whatever happened in those few missing hours was kept between the two of them. None of us asked. Seamus and Angela kept out of each other's way. The relationship between them became difficult. Angela went out more in the evenings." Looking directly at Samuel, she couldn't keep the distaste from her words. "I heard what the town said about her and I am sure our parents did, too, but Mammy never sent Seamus out to collect her again. When she did return home, sometimes the day after she left, Mammy cooked her dinner and washed her clothes. She never uttered a cross word to her, not after that day." Taking a deep breath, Deirdre sighed. "I think she knew. She must have seen something in Angela's eyes that spoke more than words could have done."

Samuel should have told her he'd heard enough but he didn't. He hungered for the truth.

"Mammy had a deep soul. She knew more than she said. She definitely knew before I did. Angela started to get sick, mostly in the mornings or when we were helping clean out the sheds. Mammy said it must be a bug she'd picked up and told me to ask Thomas to help out when he was free from his own work. He did, and I was smitten. My head was soon filled up with wedding plans, so I didn't really take any notice of the bump growing under Angela's baggy clothes. That photo you have there..." Deirdre pointed at the October picture of the unhappy looking teenager that sat on the table. "That was taken when Angela had reached her fifth month of pregnancy. The baby had started to move. It frightened her the first time. I heard her screaming to Mammy *there's an alien inside me*. Mammy held Angela's arms to stop her punching her own stomach. At first, I thought Angela wanted attention from her outburst, being that much younger than me. But one morning I walked into our room as she took off her nightgown and saw how swollen her tummy was. It was the same shape as mother's when she'd carried Angela. I cried, standing at the door seeing my baby sister carrying a babe. I cried, Samuel." Deirdre reached over and squeezed Samuel's arm. He couldn't react. He couldn't give the comfort his aunt was pleading for, so she continued.

"I don't know if the tears were from shock or annoyance that she had taken the limelight from my wedding plans or because I hadn't noticed before. I just didn't know."

Samuel stayed quiet. He could see that it pained

Deirdre to relive the past, but her words made him so angry. His mother had enjoyed the company of men from the age of thirteen and never stopped, resulting in a teenage pregnancy. Samuel thought back to his uncle, a quiet man, who he'd spent time with while growing up. He liked him, looked up to him as an honest man who seemed fair. He'd felt connected to Seamus when he started to get into trouble. The night he told Seamus he had made up his mind and packed his bags to get away from ShanInis, Seamus had taken off his flat cap, put his hand into his pocket and handed him a fist full of notes. He told Samuel to go far away from the small town, make a man of himself and return for no one. At the time, he'd thought Seamus was the only person who understood him, and yet now, he didn't know what to think.

"I was told my father left to go to America. Is that true?" Samuel demanded.

His aunt took a tissue from her pocket and blew her nose. The white of her eyes were bloodshot from holding back tears.

"No, Samuel, your father didn't leave to go to America," she answered quietly, unable to look at him.

"Is he still here in the village? Shit, did he watch me grow up and say nothing? What a bastard." Unable to sit still, he pushed his chair back, knocking it to the floor in temper. He stomped over to the stained sink, looking out to the fields and beyond, wanting nothing more than to get on a plane and leave.

"Sit down, Samuel. I won't be talking when you have your back to me."

Pushing away from the cracked sink, he reluctantly picked up the chair from the floor and sat back down, holding his head in his hands and blowing the air from his lungs.

"Go on then. Who was the sperm donor? Did she even know?" He sneered.

"What I say at this table stays at this table. Do ye understand?" She banged her fist off the wooden table top. "Delaney's do not air their sins in public. It starts and ends here." Deirdre glared, not at him but through him. The ghosts of her past echoed in the small cottage.

"Understood." Samuel leaned back in the chair, crossed his feet at his ankles and waited, folding his arms across his chest to stop his heart from pounding. He felt anything but the confident man he tried to portray.

"First, I don't want to hear a bad word about your mother from your mouth. She had troubles. We dealt with them and moved on.

"She kept this secret until the night Seamus took his own life. I found her crying in the barn. She told me the tears were happy ones and the devil should welcome him. Honestly, I didn't understand at first until she started to tell me about the night Seamus went looking for her."

Sitting forward to hear his aunt's low, trembling voice,

he reached over to hold her shaking hand.

"He had found her in the town hanging around a few boys, *like usual.* He dragged her into the car, fuming at her behaviour for everyone to see. She started to taunt him for being twenty-seven and still living at home with no girlfriend that we knew off. Angela told me she had never seen him so angry before. He kept telling her that she was a tease to all the men in the town, the way she dressed, the way she exposed her chest in the tight tops she wore. The men at The Huddle had been telling Seamus that when Angela got older, they would be waiting to have a turn. Angela said that when he'd touched her before that night, his hand would breeze past her bottom or, well, you can fill in the gaps. But that particular night he drove the car down a dark side road, pinned her down in the seat and, well, the rest was a blur but you were the result."

Samuel opened his mouth, letting out a silent scream. The realisation that his own uncle was his father made his blood boil.

"It wasn't the last time he raped her that night. All through her pregnancy, he took her innocence away, leaving her a sorrowful state."

"Wh-when did it start, the disgusting things he did to her?" He spat the words out, not wanting to be in the tainted place any longer.

"When she blossomed, she said. He wanted to touch her breasts to feel if they were real, and then he made her touch him to see his response. It still sickens me to think she had to endure him all that time and I never saw a thing. He was a quiet man, a hard working man. I thought he wasn't interested in girls."

"He wasn't. He was a sick paedophile who should have had his hands cut off and then his dick. Fuck, Deirdre, he could have interfered with other girls. Why did she wait so long to tell anyone?"

"Secrets and lies, Samuel. We all have them. Some are bigger than others, but most we take to our graves."

"The whole thing is sick. This house should be burnt to the ground."

"This house is yours. When Seamus's will was read, everything he owned belonged to Angela. The house, his money, everything. He signed over most of the land the day she left this house and moved into town when she turned seventeen and not when your grandparents passed away. Looking back, after his passing I think he paid for her rent there, too. That was what some of the receipts showed anyway. She didn't want this house. Her memories were not happy here, so she signed it straight over to you. She really hoped ye would come back home."

"Seriously, Deirdre, I can't have this cottage now. I loved that man but what he did... I hate him. I fucking hate him."

"He loved you. I think he knew you were his. Were ye happy in this house, Samuel, when you visited?"

"This place held all my happy memories, but now every one of them is destroyed."

"Keep the house, Sam. History won't change but the future can."

"Why are you telling me all this now?"

"Samuel, your mother's passing and how you handled it made me realise that you needed to know why she lived her life the way she did. You reminded her every day of what had happened to her, how everything turned upside down. I'm not condoning how she treated ye for a second, but you needed to understand why. It wasn't my place to tell ye while she had breath in her body."

"I need to get out of here." Without waiting for Deirdre's permission, Samuel pulled the door open and walked to the hire car parked around the front. He held onto the steering wheel, banged his head against the headrest, and cursed as the tears he didn't want, fell freely down his cheeks.

Twenty Six

Samuel didn't know how long he sat in the car. Time had ceased to exist the moment his aunt had sat down at the table to confess. So many questions floated around his brain but none he wanted to hear the answers to – not today, not tomorrow, maybe never. The note he found stuck on the inside of the box now made sense. The handwritten words, he realised, were from his mother, read *the truth will be revealed in time, Samuel's father will be exposed.*

He should have started the car, disappeared down the boreen and kept driving, but with the temper burning inside his blood, he couldn't trust himself to survive the journey. For years, he'd kept his uncle on a pedestal – a father figure, a trusted man, now tainted in his memory for what he'd done.

The car door opened, and the breeze flowed through the vehicle. Even with his eyes closed, he knew the fragrance belonged to Faye.

"What are you doing here?" Irritated, he wanted to drown in his own company.

"Your aunt told me where you were."

The door closed and Samuel sighed, knowing Faye had joined him in the car. He rubbed his temple as the throbbing pain pushed its way to the surface.

"I thought we weren't talking, remember?"

"We're talking. I'm just pissed off with you."

"What do you want, Faye?" Samuel demanded. Secrets should be kept, should die with the people that hid them for so long. He was pissed off that the secret now belonged to him. It was too late to do anything about it, too late to resolve what should have been dealt with more than thirty odd years ago.

"I came to help at the cottage."

"Why?" The single word had looped around and around his confused mind more than once since he'd stepped off the plane.

"Because you are a friend and I like it here."

"I'm thinking of giving the house up to Dee."

"Wha...Why? It is a beautiful place. Don't give it up. You can't."

Samuel turned his pounding head to face Faye. Her cheeks were red from walking. To him, she was the most beautiful girl in the world, but he couldn't have the ugly truth hanging over him.

"We are good friends, aren't we? We were good lovers,

too. It seems there's a good reason why I am so fucked up."

"You have always been fucked up, Samuel. That was why I fell in love with you in the first place. It's the silent treatment I find hard to deal with. When you stop talking to me, block me out of your life – that is what pisses me off. That is the reason we aren't together right now."

"And if you knew the reason why I am this way, would you take me back?"

"I'm unable to answer that right now, not until I know why."

"Let's get out of here, but not in this fecking steel cage."

Samuel got out of the car and waited for Faye to do the same. She wanted the truth, so he was going to give it to her. Every last drop of it.

Taking long strides, he headed to the kitchen of the main house. Dee was sitting at the table cradling the baby while her mother heated up a bottle for his feed.

"Deirdre, does Thomas still have the Honda in the shed?" Samuel asked from the door, not wanting to step inside.

"He does," she answered, surprised.

"Working okay still?"

"It was last time he took it out."

"Do you have the keys?"

"Hanging up by the front door on the key rack."

"Gear with it?"

"Helmets are still in the shed, yes."

"Petrol?"

"In the tank, I guess."

"I'm going to take Faye out on it. Is that okay with you?"

"Where are ye going?"

"Probably to Land's Head up at the point. There is a new café there," Samuel told her. Seeing her preparing the feed for Tadgh, he couldn't stay mad with her. Deirdre wasn't to blame for the tragedy that had happened in that cottage, but it didn't stop him from being angry.

"There is. It's been open for a while now. You would know these things if you came home."

"You know who owns it, don't you?" Dee asked, cranking her head around to Samuel as waited for the bottle from her mother.

"No. Who?"

"That O'Brien family at the pub. They have their granddaughter working there."

"She is a bit young for that," Deirdre stated, shaking the warm bottle in her hand.

"Twelve or thirteen, I think. She only helps out, Mam, nothing illegal and no different from us working in the fields helping Da."

"Are you saying she is Molly's kid?" As the words left his mouth, realisation started to hit him.

"Think she is. Ye remember Molly, don't you?"

"Yeah, Dee, I remember Molly. Faye and I are staying at the pub."

"So you must have bumped into her."

"We have, briefly."

"Why don't you stay here with us now you are talking to Mam. It would make sense, wouldn't it?" Dee tested the milk on the back of her hand, now she had the bottle before Tadgh drank the warm milk greedily.

"That's Samuel's choice. I'm sure he doesn't want to put us out with the babe and all," the older woman answered, retreating back to the sink to fill up the kettle, turning her back to the room.

"I like my sleep, Dee, and that little mite on your lap, I'm sure, does not." He shot a glance at his aunt, watching her moving about to make drinks. He sure as hell did not intend to bring up the subject of his mother in front of his cousin, and Deirdre, with her eyes on anything but him, looked like she didn't want to either. "I'll just grab those keys and be off."

Samuel took the set of keys from the hook and joined Faye outside where she was waiting in the late summer warmth. Catching her hand as he walked by, he steered her towards the shed, holding on firmly. It didn't go unnoticed that Faye didn't try to move her hand away from his, and that small gesture made his lips curve upward. Faye stood close while he unlocked the shed door and pulled the cover off the midnight blue motorbike. Checking the array of jackets, boots, helmets and gloves, Samuel found a small size for Faye and a larger size for him.

"Why does your uncle have so much gear?" Faye asked, hopping on one leg to push her foot into the boot.

"He used to work for a bike school as an instructor. He kind of gathered a few bits and pieces along the way."

"Is that where you learnt?"

"Yeah, Uncle Thomas is a sound man."

"Sound man? What does that mean?"

"Sound, as in honest, cool, one of a kind."

"Oh right. It would be nice to meet him."

"Yeah, you will, hopefully. He is a busy man. I guess the silage season has kept him from the house."

"Okay, now you have to explain silage..."

"Later. Now it's time to ride."

Zipping up the leather jacket, Samuel handed over a helmet to Faye. Out of the corner of his eye, he watched the way she looked at him. She thought he didn't see and it made him feel excited but guilty. Soon they would be enjoying a well-needed coffee overlooking the Atlantic Ocean and he would be telling her things he didn't want to. Would she hate him when she knew? Was this the beginning of the end?

The ride along the coastline with its twists and turns made Samuel feel like he was eighteen again. Carefree, daring, youthful, he didn't want the journey to end. The breeze filtering through his jacket cooled his temper and dulled the pain in his head. Faye's arms wound around his waist, making him wish they could head to the coast and fumble under a picnic blanket like teenagers.

Pulling up in the car park, he turned off the engine and spent a few minutes savouring the closeness of Faye's body to his. Her arms were still wrapped around his waist, and he enjoyed the sound of her breathing, accelerated from the ride.

He signalled to Faye that she could get off the bike, now he had it steady between his thighs. He followed suit, taking off his helmet and leaving it on the bars of the bike. Holding her hand, he guided her across the road to the viewing point. It didn't surprise him that she was oohing and aahing. It was a common reaction to the sight of the Atlantic Ocean.

"Come closer. I want to get a photo with the view in the background," Faye said, taking out her phone and setting up the camera app.

"You know what, if, when we come out of the café, you still want a photo, then I will."

"Okay, but would you take some of me before we go in?" she asked, her head cocked to the side waiting for his answer.

Samuel held out his hand, taking the phone while Faye got herself into position. After taking four pictures, he handed it back and made his way to the café, disheartened that those pictures might hold sad memories for Faye in the near future.

The young girl that served him before was absent this time and Samuel felt a little relieved. He didn't want to face his new responsibility while trying to explain his fucked up life. That could wait for another day – a day he doubted would happen.

He ordered a bacon bagel and a large coffee, remembering he had missed breakfast that morning. Faye ordered the same and they took a seat at the back of the café overlooking the sea.

"How did you get to the cottage this morning, did you walk all the way?" Samuel wanted to keep the chat light while waiting for their order to arrive.

"I walked to the town to see some stalls I'd missed, and halfway around I met Dee with Tadgh. She drove me up afterwards."

"I didn't think I would see you today," he confessed, realising how much he'd missed having Faye around him.

"Not all of us hold grudges, Sam. Anyway, it was Dee who convinced me."

"Did she? You needed convincing then?"

"We were talking and I told her about last night in the bar, how mad I was with you and that poor guy who got to know your fist too well."

"And what did she say?"

"That you had a troubled past that you were trying to deal with. Although you've given me an inkling, I'm guessing there is much more yet to tell."

"You're right, there is, but even Dee doesn't know everything."

"I told her if you would talk more then maybe you wouldn't have such a troubled future."

"Well, it seems that between the two of you I have been sussed."

"Her baby is cute."

"Are you serious? I thought you didn't *do* babies."

"I don't but he is cute."

"Did she tell you he isn't hers?"

"Yeah, I think she is a much better woman than I could ever be. If that was my sister, I would have put my foot down."

The conversation paused when the food arrived and Samuel inhaled the caffeine he'd missed out on earlier.

"This is good food," Faye managed to say between mouthfuls of the warm bagel.

Samuel finished his food and pushed his plate away. Leaving the unused knife and fork on the side, he waited for Faye to do the same.

Sipping his coffee slowly, he savoured the taste. The time had come to confess. He could see the bottom of the mug and wished the coffee would fill up again to give him more time. Once the truth was out, he would know if he had lost her.

"Faye, what I am going to tell you isn't easy for me.

The person you see in front of you has tried to do the best he could with the little he had. I have never stopped loving you. In the ten years, we have been together you have made me complete. I don't want to lose that, but I understand it hasn't been easy for you in the past few months. I totally get why you sent the text to end it. I wouldn't have changed if you hadn't. I'm not into all that counselling shit, but maybe it was the kick up the arse I needed."

Samuel paused while he waited for the waiter to take the plates, ordering another coffee before he left because he needed something to occupy his restless hands. Faye stayed silent, and he was thankful for that. If she had started to talk, he didn't think he would have been able to continue. When the filled mug arrived and he'd said his thanks, Faye took his outstretched hand in hers across the table.

"Okay, right, here goes. Hope you are ready for this. You know my aunt and uncle brought me up. I told you my mother died when I was young back when we first met. I'm sorry that I lied. I'm sorry that when I left the café that morning, I never told you the reason why I lied. I was angry, angry with *her* for being in my life again when things were going so well. Telling you about *her* meant she had a part in my life and that would have been fucking bad. To me, she died the day I was taken away."

Samuel looked out of the window to view the calm sea, not wanting to be in the room anymore. He never felt comfortable talking about his past and avoided it at all costs, but losing Faye was a cost he didn't want to pay. Even as friends, he wanted her.

"She drank a lot. When she wasn't sleeping or fucking, she was drinking," he confessed to the sea. "I was the kid who got in the way, but I was a free ticket to money. The government paid for the roof over our heads. My existence kept her in food. But the best money came from the men who supplied her with drink. Their money, she said more than once, kept her sane. She had a temper." He scoffed. "I guess the apple didn't fall far from the tree there. I don't know how it happened but at the age of seven, I was placed in Deirdre's home, for good. I guess you can say the rest is history." Samuel moved his hand away from Faye's and started to drink his second coffee of the day, needing to stop talking. Telling Faye the truth wasn't easy but telling her the whole truth, about his mother, seemed impossible.

"I don't know what to say, Sam."

"I don't want you to say anything. I'd be fucking happy if we never spoke about this again after today."

He took another mouthful of coffee before placing the mug on the table and wiping his forehead as he inhaled the scent of Faye's perfume. The flowery aroma dispersed the bitter taste from his mouth that speaking about his mother left him with.

"You remember the letter that arrived the morning you were late?"

"How could I not? It was the start of this downward

238

spiral."

"Yeah, it fucked up everything. Deirdre sent it. Angie was in hospital and she wanted me to come over. Not for visiting but to sort out paperwork at the hospital. Apparently, my name was down as next of kin. Me!"

"Maybe she had no one else. Did you think of that?"

"Maybe she got too old to keep her legs open for all those men."

"Samuel! That's your mother you are talking about."

"And? Am I meant to forget everything she put me through? The beatings? Being starved? Fuck, that woman made my life hell."

Samuel rubbed the sweat from his palms on his thighs. The air in the café had become thick and he wanted to get back on the bike and ride to the end of the world. He would have done if it hadn't been for Faye sitting opposite.

"I pushed you away because of her. I never thought that would happen. I waited until the last moment to go over, met with the doctors, signed the paperwork and left as fast as I could. Deirdre was mad because of my decision, but to me, it was the only thing she deserved."

"What did you do, Sam?"

"I didn't kill her if that is what you think. The machine keeping her alive had to be turned off and I had to give the go ahead for any healthy organs to be donated."

Faye clasped her hand over her mouth. Samuel hadn't intended to shock her or cause tears to well up in her eyes, but he had. He wondered whether he should leave out the part where he'd gone against Angie's wishes and wanted to send her body to research, but he told her that, too.

He didn't have to see the look on Faye's face after he spoke. He could hear in her sobs that she thought he had been a total bastard. He got up from his chair and approached the counter, taking some serviettes and a glass of water back to the seat for her. He waited for her to compose herself, watching as she wiped away the black mascara that had streamed down her face. He knew why she couldn't look at him, yet he continued.

"I never knew the cottage had been left to her. None of it made sense. Why would her brother leave the place to her and then to me? And then I learned what I found out this morning. My father, who I was always told had left to find riches in America, was, in fact, my Uncle Seamus, her fucking brother. How fucking sick is that?"

Faye pushed her chair away from the table, spilling the water as she did. Samuel stood up, but she held her hand out to him, shaking her head with the other over her mouth. She had turned as pale as snow and he had to let her leave, give her the space she deserved.

He cleared up the water on the table using the napkins. From where he stood he could see the pathway leading to the viewing point. He watched Faye lean against the stone wall, her hair wild in the ocean breeze. Using her hand, she held it away from her face, and Samuel could see the pain etched there. Feeling helpless, he knew he had lost her. His truth had made her run, just as he'd known it would but foolishly hoped it wouldn't.

He paid for their breakfast then joined her outside, standing a little distance away.

"One thing you can't hate me for is that view," he said, needing reassurance that they were still at least on speaking terms.

"I want to go back to the hotel."

Samuel nodded, but inside he fumed at himself. One thing he had learnt from his aunt was that the truth should stay hidden until the day you die, and right now, he felt like he had died and gone to hell.

Twenty Seven

After dropping Faye off at The Huddle, Samuel went to the nearest gas station and filled the bike up with petrol. He intended to use every drop to sort out his brain before he returned.

The scenic ride filled his lungs with the smell of the country and his visor caught every small fly that got in his way. He didn't stop until his stomach began to shout at him, and then he reluctantly turned the bike around and rode back.

Even he was surprised when he pulled up at the cottage. He hadn't consciously thought about where he would go. What surprised him more was that when he entered the kitchen, the place looked cleaner than he'd left it, and Faye was sitting at the kitchen table looking at photographs with his Aunt Deirdre.

"Am I interrupting something?" he asked, wondering what the fuck he had walked in on.

"Dee collected Faye earlier. We had some talking to

do."

"Oh, and are you finished? Should I leave?"

"We are. I'm showing Faye you as a grumpy teenager," she said, waving an old picture in her hand.

"Who waved a magic wand over this room?"

"That was both of us. We thought you would need somewhere to at least eat from," Deirdre replied.

"Is there any food?" He was stunned by the surreal scene before him.

"You never lost it. Even as a kid, he thought only of his stomach and what he could put in it," Deirdre explained to Faye. "There is a lasagne cooking in the main house. Wait here and I'll bring it down," she said, turning her attention to Samuel who felt like he'd ridden into a parallel universe where nothing made sense.

"I'll help." Faye began to get up from her seat. Samuel looked between his aunt and the girlfriend he had lost.

"No, sit, Faye. Ye two have unfinished business to sort out."

Samuel waited until his aunt was out of earshot before approaching the table and taking her vacant seat.

"What the fuck is going on?"

"Do you realise how much this family loves you? Do you? I am sorry I was so pissed off with you in the café. You're cold hearted at times and it grates on me. You were one of the lucky ones who got out of a very bad situation young enough to have years with such a great family. Did you ever think about that in all your woes?"

Samuel let the words sink into his stubborn brain, fighting with a headache that was winning. He'd lived with Deirdre and her family for longer than he'd spent with his own mother, and yet he'd let her problems hang over him all that time. Only now did the magnitude of what his aunt had done for him hit him.

"What kind of man have I turned out to be?" The words spilled out, shattering him. Lowering his head until his chin rested on his chest, he clasped his fingers around the back of his neck.

"Only you can change that. Deirdre has filled me in on what you left out. Those nightmares you have relate to your past, don't you think?"

"I don't fucking know what to think anymore," he confessed, the heavy weight of the words hanging in the air.

"Sam, this is your life. You are thirty-three years old. Don't you think it is time to start living? Your mother behaved appallingly but she had her reasons. Her brother raped her, not once but several times. Do you have any idea what that does to a woman and her soul? Especially when it is compressed inside and kept secret. Your uncle... father killed himself, taking that to his grave. Did he feel guilty? Only he could answer that, but after what he did, I'll bet he did. This cottage is yours, this is your family and honestly, I think you are one lucky fucker to have them." Faye stamped her small fist on the table with the last word, and

Samuel closed his eyes, not wanting to see the bastard he had become.

"Deirdre really has filled you in with everything. Did she tell you what is said at this table stays at this table?" he asked quietly.

"Yes, and that is why we are sitting here now talking about it. I don't want either of us to leave until all the truth is out. Is it out now, Sam?" He could feel Faye's eyes boring into him and opened his to meet them. They were wide and mad.

"Yes, well, no, there is one more thing, but you will hate it," he confessed.

"Well, it can join the list of all the other things I hate, can't it?" she spat out, crossing her arms across her chest.

"Fuck, I swear I only heard this last night at the bar, before I threw that punch." Taking a lungful of air, he knew the only way to tell her was fast and then deal with the fallout.

"The redhead in the bar, Molly... We had a thing years ago, and I mean years ago, but you know that already. I was young, and well before I left, we took things one step further than ever before. I swear it only happened the once in a moment of madness and we didn't use protection. I pulled out before... well, you know how it is done. I left. I presumed she'd carried on at school and followed her plans to go to Dublin and study, which she did. What I never knew until yesterday was that I left more behind than I should have. She was pregnant, Faye. I swear to God I had no idea and no-one told me." He lifted his head and wiped his hands down his face and around his neck, blowing the air from his lungs.

"And the child? What happened to it?" Her question sounded cold to his ears.

"She had a girl and named her Niamh. After her studies, she married a man called Steve and they are still very much together now." He hoped his answer sounded uninterested.

"So why is she working behind the bar?"

"She came down for the weekend to help out, and... our daughter stays here during the summer months. The festival brought them both back here for the weekend. The Huddle and the café where we went today belong to her parents."

"Shit, Sam, you are a father."

"I'm a sperm donor, nothing more than that."

"You have to make contact and be in Niamh's life."

"Why? I haven't been in it so far."

"Don't you get it? It is like history repeating itself. You have to let your daughter decide if she wants you in her life, not you." Samuel knew from the way Faye was speaking that she was mentally working out how.

"But you don't like children. I don't want to lose you any more than I already have." Holding out his hand, he wanted to feel a connection, any connection he could make with Faye. She rested her hand in his. It was small and warm in comparison.

"Nothing is simple in life, Sam. I have learnt that much in the past few days. You need to sort out where you should be in your daughter's life and maybe then we can sort out where we are."

Samuel held on tight to her words. He selfishly wanted Faye back in his life, all of her.

"We have got this, Faye, me and you. No one else exists when I am with you."

"Promise me one thing. Don't take too long. I have missed you."

"Fly back with me on the next plane. Let's leave and go home."

"Sam, no. Haven't you listened to a word I have said? Your daughter, your aunt, your mother, your uncle, you need to deal with them all. Only then can you go home."

Samuel got up and walked to where Faye sat. Standing by her, he held out his hands and waited for her to take them, lifting one eyebrow to encourage her. Faye smiled back at him and rested her fingertips in his palms. Pulling her to standing, he enclosed the only woman he truly loved in his arms, needing to feel her heartbeat pounding next to his. Tenderly, he brushed away a piece of hair that covered her face. He leant down and gently left three quick kisses on her forehead – one for the past, one for the present and one for the future he wanted with her. Stopping, he looked down to her gazing eyes, which were clouded with tears.

"Oh, sweetheart, don't you get it? There is no sorting out. Both of my parents are dead. I don't have their guilt hanging over me. And the child... Well, she lives in Dublin and I don't." He shrugged his shoulders, trying to see what was behind her glazed eyes. "None of these things will get in our way." He smiled.

Faye bit down on her plump bottom lip, and the tears started to flow down her cheeks. Samuel could feel her hands trembling in his before she pulled them away.

"No, no, no, Faye. No, don't do this." Samuel tried to grab her hands back. Stepping away, she rushed to the other side of the table, out of his reach.

Samuel didn't move. For that brief moment, he'd thought things were going back to how they had been before the letter.

"Talk to me, babe. What did I say wrong? I don't get it."

Faye held onto the back of a chair, her face stained from the tears that refused to stop. Wiping the back of her hand over her nose, she sniffed and reached for a tissue from her pocket. She cleared her sniffles and regained herself enough to look at him again.

"You...You disgust me, Sam." The eyes he had fallen for years ago narrowed. "Find a fucking heart," she spat at him, her words quivering.

"I have a heart, babe. It's just different," he threw back

at her across the table.

"You are an arsehole, Samuel Walsh or Delaney, whoever you are. I don't even know you."

"I am the same man you knew ten years ago."

"I think you are right. Maybe I have been blind all this time. You are a cold hearted fucker and if it had been me in that hospital, I bet you would have done the same thing."

Faye threw her hand over her mouth. Samuel could hardly hear the words she mumbled behind them. His feet moved faster than his brain and within four large steps, he had her in his arms, carrying her through the cottage to the bedroom once occupied by his uncle.

Pushing the contents of the boxes from earlier off the bed, he lay Faye down on the bumpy mattress then stood at the side of the bed, his fists clenched tight. She sat up and pulled her legs to her chest, wrapping her arms around them. He could hear her sob as she buried her face in her knees.

"You. Are. Nothing. Like. Angie. I'd take your place rather than see you die. Don't ever think you are like her. Do you hear me? Do you?" he roared.

Turning to face the wall of the bedroom, he pulled back his arm and punched the peeling paint. Again and again, he hit the wall, splitting the skin on his knuckles. Dark red blood splattered on the wooden floor as he shook the pain from his already bruised hand, flexing his fingers and closing them again. Samuel looked around the floor and found a piece of old cloth to wrap around his hand, to stop the blood.

Faye moved from the bed and sat on the edge. "Show me," she said, her tears reduced to a damp patch on her cheeks, her voice all but a whisper.

Samuel kneeled down in front of her, his arm out for her to inspect. He kept his eyes on the floor.

"Look at me, Sam."

He did what she asked and shamefully raised his eyes to meet hers.

"Don't ever shout at me again. You need to see someone when you get home. You scared me."

"I wouldn't hurt you. You know that, don't you?" he pleaded.

"I...I think talking to someone will help. There is a lot of shit going on in that head of yours."

Faye unwrapped the cloth and patted Samuel's knuckles, clearing up the blood drying around the grazes, the old wounds opened with the new. She waited for his reaction. He licked his dry lips, his anger still hovering beneath the surface.

"I'm not seeing a shrink. I'm not fucking mad."

"I didn't say you were."

"It's not right, lying on a couch and all that shit."

"If you don't at least try then that temper of yours is going to get out of control."

"I can't lose you, Faye."

"Then sort this shit out. I'm going to book a ticket home, and I don't want to hear from you until you are ready to be the man you should be."

"Don't go, Faye. Stay here with me, please," he pleaded.

"I'll only cloud your thoughts and keep you from doing what is right. Go, have time with your daughter, say goodbye to your mother properly, and make peace with your family."

"If I had known where that letter would lead, I would have burnt it."

"Nothing can be hidden for long. Nothing, Samuel, remember that."

Twenty Eight

Faye refused Samuel's offer of a lift to the airport that evening, accepting one from Dee instead. She was grateful her goodbyes were brief. Samuel leaned in and kissed her goodbye – a kiss that would be the last one for a long time. His hand was wrapped in a bandage bought from the chemist in the town.

Faye handed him a handwritten note, folded neatly into an envelope along with a small parting gift wrapped in tissue paper. She'd told him he wasn't to open it until he was ready to come home. Samuel promised he wouldn't, but Faye knew realistically it could take weeks, months even, and the last piece of her heart shattered. As the car pulled away from the curb, she lifted her hand to wave goodbye, not knowing whether he would come back to her once he got to know his daughter and family again.

For so long, Faye had been his family, his only love, but now things had changed, for better or worse.

Dee drove the car, talking about the different stalls in

the town over the weekend. Faye knew she was trying to disperse the heavy cloud that was hanging in the air. She listened to Samuel's cousin, explaining which shops had been around when he'd lived there before. She couldn't help but stay silent as the surreal world played out around her.

"He will come back to you, Faye," Dee told her as the airport came into view. "Don't give up on him."

Faye couldn't answer her. She didn't know if she could without lying. The envelope she had handed to Samuel might be faded and lost by the time he returned, and Faye would be a distant memory, just the way Ireland had been before his return.

It was like history repeating itself, but this time, Ireland would claim him back.

After hugging Dee goodbye at the drop-off point, Faye entered the small airport with only one thought in her mind.

Was this was the beginning of their end.

THE END

Footnote:

A boreen is a little road, a country lane, or a narrow frequently unpaved, rural road in Ireland.

ShanInis:

Fictional Irish name meaning Shan~Old

Inish~island, water meadow.

Coilín:

Irish word used for girl

The Irish Law on donor cards:

All organ donations in Ireland are coordinated through the Irish Organ Procurement Office at Beaumont Hospital. Strict ethical guidelines protect the interests of organ donors, their families and transplant recipients, and anonymity is maintained regarding the identity of the donor and recipients.

If you wish to become an organ donor after your death, you should inform your next-of-kin of your intentions. In Ireland, consent is never presumed, even if a donor card has been signed. Your next-of-kin would always be consulted and asked for consent in order for donation to proceed.

Acknowledgements

I want to thank Heather for her patience and talent for editing my book. You make my words take flight all in the right order.

Laura Hampton, thank you.

To Jo who may never know how much she means to me. She keeps me sane when my mind is going loopy.

The amazing group of ladies from Hooked on Books Cherry Promotions on helping with the release of Hidden and all that is involved in the preparations ie me messaging a lot!
https://www.facebook.com/hookedonbookspromotionso5/

Leigh, from Irish Ink, who sprinkled her formatting

magic over my pages to make them pretty.

To the wonderful JC Clarke, thank you for making a cover I fell in love with the minute I saw it. The story blossomed and the model became Samuel.

To my beta readers, Jo, Dawn, and LJ who were the first to read through my raw story and give me the encouragement I needed to progress. Your input was extremely valuable.

To L Chapman, thank you for being patient with me. My questions, uncertainty, and rambles never made you block me and for that, I am truly grateful.

My playlist, without all the songs singing in my head, taking me to a place to let me write, my emotions would still be mixed up.

And to you, the reader.

Without you books would be left on shelves getting dusty, eBooks would never be downloaded and a writer's imagination would have no escape.

Thank you

My words, emotions, and imagination are in your

hands.

> To read is to dream
>
> To read erotic is to fantasise
>
> To read romance is to breathe life into your heart.

About the Author

Leaving the bright lights of London behind in the early 90's, Amelia J Hunter is an indie writer who lives in the Irish countryside with her family, a good coffee maker and plenty of fresh air.

Hidden is the first of the Uncovered stories.

Website: https://www.ameliajhunter.blogspot.ie

Mail to: ameliajhunter1@gmail.com

Twitter: https://twitter.com/ameliajhunter1

Facebook:
https://www.facebook.com/profile.php?id=100004854377260&ref=ts&fref=ts

Goodreads:
https://www.goodreads.com/book/show/31279277-hidden

Made in the USA
Charleston, SC
18 September 2016